Eligible Ex-husband

MARIE JOHNSTON

LE PUBLISHING

Developmental and Line editing by Angela James

Copy editing by My Brother's Editor

Proofreading by: My Brother's Editor, Angel Nyx, and Fairy Proof Mother

Cover by Sarah Kil Creative Studio

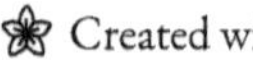 Created with Vellum

The man in the magazine spread, the one dubbed the most eligible bachelor, is my ex-husband.

Six months ago, Simon's company was never more successful, just like our marriage was never emptier. I was a stay-at-home mom with a sugar daddy who had no time to pass the sugar or be a daddy. I asked for a divorce and he let me go, just like that.

Now, I'm mending my broken heart and finding myself while being a strong role model for our girls. But when my mom gets sick, I need help, and he's there like a superhero in a tailored suit. And when my mom recovers, he's still there, doing grocery runs and braiding our girls' hair.

I don't want to hang my hopes on my workaholic ex just because he's suddenly wearing basketball shorts instead of designer threads or because he's giving me that look that melted my heart in college.

Chemistry was never our problem. I don't want to trust that he's changed only to find out that, once again, I'm not worth fighting for. He needs to prove that he'll be as ruthless about us as he is in the boardroom.

One

Natalie

Discovering who was deemed North Dakota's most eligible bachelor ruined my morning. The article streams through my head like a Netflix show I can't turn off, only there's no pause asking me if I want to keep watching.

My best friend Rachel forwarded a link to me this morning, hoping to spare me from discovering the news in line at the grocery store. There he was in a full-page spread. Handsome, with a chiseled jaw and naturally highlighted dirty-blond hair, a body honed by years on the rowing team in high school—which had most definitely *not* been in North Dakota—and a net worth in the millions. All self-made. And, of course, they included the part about his brother's sudden death three years ago. It was right before describing him as the doting dad of two little girls and commenting on how he successfully co-parented with his ex-wife.

I snort and thrust my legs up. The metal plates of the leg

press clang against the top and I ease my legs back down to a count of four. My quads are burning.

"Still thinking about that garbage?" My personal trainer peers over me, her hair pulled off her face in braided rows, mirth glittering in her eyes. I gave her the article when I arrived and told her to work me so hard I'd forget all about it.

"Yes," I hiss and strain upward with my legs once more, my muscles shaking like a newly birthed calf. I have three more reps to go.

"You want to quit leg day a little early so we can go for a run?"

My next yes comes out in a puff as I push my legs straight.

Aleah keeps talking, doing her best to motivate me. Cheering me up, but not so much helping me forget. "You'd think running would give you too much time to dwell on all those ladies and gentlemen who'll be drooling over the full-body shot of Mr. North Dakota in a Tom Ford, but the endorphins help you care a whole lot less."

I somehow doubt that I can cover enough ground to not care. "I can't let it ruin my whole day. It was just so unexpected. Wake up, it's a normal day. Then... that." A reminder of everything I've lost in bold-faced type.

Aleah crosses her arms, her sleek and defined biceps flexing. Every arm day, I look at her bare arms to get me through the endless sets of push-ups she makes me do. "That sucks, Nat. And you know it's okay to be angry, right?"

I finish my last rep and grab a drink from my water bottle. Time for the run. "I am angry." I wipe my brow with a gym towel. "I thought I was over it. I *should* be over it."

She tsks. "Don't should on yourself. What's my rule?"

"No shoulding myself during training." I suck in a long breath. She's right. This gym has become my mecca. A positive environment. Moving meditation, Aleah calls it. I need some of that now.

I stash my items in the locker room and follow Aleah outside. It's a pleasant morning for a run. There's enough wind to hold the onslaught of sweat at bay and it's early June, so the bugs aren't out en masse quite yet. Birds chirp and hop around the parking lot between cars. They scatter as we walk by. Aleah and I go to the end of the sidewalk where the running path loops by the gym.

I don't know how many clients she runs with, but it isn't like going with me taxes her stamina any. Half the time, I swear she's trying hard not to walk right next to me as I slog full speed ahead.

She's right, though. After the first half mile, my give a shit starts to taper slowly downward.

A fitness watch is shoved in my face and I try to focus without face-planting on the pavement.

"Look at your time. You've improved so much." Aleah goes back to barely moving while I die a little with each step.

Six months ago, I sought out a personal trainer with the determination to fix myself. I was newly single and too comfortable in my identity as a frumpy mom. In college, I had such big plans. Now, thirty's on the horizon and other than my accomplishment of birthing tiny humans and making sure they hit all their milestones, I don't have anything else to claim.

Nothing. I gave it all up. The kids are going off to school. Then what? Who am I? What kind of role model do I want to be? Who is Natalie Underwood?

"Whoa." Aleah breaks into my thoughts. "You must be chewing on that article. This'll be your best pace ever."

I don't slow down. It feels good to release the burn inside me. "I found my motivation."

"Do you think he knew about the article?" Aleah circles

her finger, letting me know that we'll be turning around where the running trail intersects with a street.

For once, I wasn't thinking about what I read, but my pace kicked up talking about it. "He had to. Someone had to take the pictures." Pictures of North Dakota's most eligible bachelor looking tall, fit, and dead sexy.

The unfairness of it all.

We run back in silence, my angry pace fading with my energy.

The gym comes into view. The parking lot has several cars in it, but one in particular stands out. A sleek silver ride with a striking man getting out, unfolding his long frame. He flips his suit jacket and buttons it as he shoots the building a hard stare. A gorgeous, willowy blond is in the front seat, clicking through a phone. The man rounds the car, his shoulders impressively broad in his expensive suit. His expression is shadowed, like even the sun is too impressed to shine too brightly on him.

His gaze lands on me and his jaw tightens. It's the only expression I ever see on him anymore.

"Is that..." Awe fills Aleah's voice. She's my biggest cheerleader, but I always feel like it's hard to truly impress her. Of course, that's easy for him too.

"Yes." I sigh and slow to a walk so I won't be gasping by the time I reach him.

The back door of the sedan opens and a sandy-blond head pops out. Abigail. She prefers Abby.

She grins and waves with all the energy of an eight-year-old. "Hey, Mom!"

I wave back. Why would my luck change today? Sweat drips down my neck and soaks my hair. My face is probably stoplight red and these gray capri leggings highlight every dimple in my thighs. The gym is supposed to be my safe zone, the place where I can put the pieces of me back together again.

Instead, I'm literally a hot mess and the man I can't quit thinking about is heading my way. The man I thought I'd be with long past forever. The only man I'm afraid I'll ever want to be with at all. North Dakota's most eligible bachelor. My ex-husband.

* * *

Simon

My ex-wife looks *fucking* amazing.

For the thousandth time, I wonder where the hell we went wrong. Simon and Natalie. She goes by Nat with everyone else. We even gave our girls nicknames because I once told Natalie that I wished I had a nickname growing up. I thought we were the strongest couple ever. We both graduated college with a small baby and moved to another state to start a business together.

Now we're divorced. And she's been busting ass to get into shape, though there's never been anything wrong with her shape at any point in her life. I stay awake too long at night ruminating about her motivation. My subtle attempts to get the girls to reveal whether or not Natalie is seeing anyone without outright asking have failed.

The lady running next to her has a rueful tilt to her lips. "Well, if it isn't North Dakota's most eligible bachelor."

That stupid lifestyle piece turned out to be more entertainment than informative. It was my executive assistant's idea and since Helena's had nothing but golden nuggets since I hired her, I went with it. Whether it's going to be the type of exposure I want is undetermined, but the way Natalie's eyes narrow on me like I'm a potential mugger says no.

I give the other woman a congenial smile. "And you must be..."

Natalie answers. "This is Aleah, my personal trainer."

The rising tide of suspicion swells. She's even hired a personal trainer? The girls told me this is her gym since Natalie doesn't share those details anymore. When we were married, I didn't think she even knew gyms existed. But from Natalie's vibrant glow, the training's going well.

I'm happy for her and doesn't that make me want to disassemble the entire gym and take it to the landfill? She used to be happy with me.

But I play the nice guy. Fargo is small enough that I can't tarnish my image as a business owner. I extend my hand. "Aleah, nice to meet you. Simon."

"Oh, I know." She gives my hand a quick squeeze and chortles in a way that lets me know she's fully Team Natalie.

Aleah gives Natalie's arm a squeeze. "Don't forget to stretch. See you Thursday."

Natalie nods, her gaze dropping. I take the opportunity to soak her in. She has her rusty-brown, riotous hair pulled back in a ponytail, but it looks like she kissed an electrical socket. Our five-year-old daughter Maddy got her hair. It's lighter like mine but uncontrollably curly like Natalie's.

"What are you doing here?" Natalie's stare is wary and I hate that I'm the reason for it. Especially since she has every right to think this isn't a simple visit.

"I have to go out of town," I say.

"So?"

She isn't going to make it easy. "I'm dropping the girls off."

"Simon." Can she sound more disappointed? "All they asked for was a week with you after school ended. You said you'd work from home, or they could be in the office with you."

"We have all of summer vacation to get a week in."

"*No*, they have swimming lessons and sports camps and playdates with friends." Her gaze strays to the car where Helena's arranging a plane and hotel rooms. Nostrils flaring, she says, "Take them with you."

I couldn't have heard her correctly. "Natalie, be serious."

"I am. It's your week. I have things to do."

"Like what?" I have no right to ask, but I'm insatiably curious about what she's been doing since she quit working for the company and this is the perfect excuse to ask.

"I'm training."

"I can see that." I meant to keep the wry tone out of my voice. It's something that pissed her off to no end in the year before she sprang the divorce on me.

Her scowl deepens. "I have online training. For a job," she finished defensively.

My brows pop up. She's going back to work? When we graduated and opened Underwood Equity, we agreed that she'd perform assistant duties but otherwise be the primary stay-at-home parent and we'd live off mac 'n' cheese until the business took off. Those years had stretched out until my brother died and left me money. That money that bought the house I no longer live in and was the jump-start my business needed. I've worked three times harder than ever since to make Underwood Equity what it should be.

It's all I have left of Hayes.

Natalie walked away from the company when she walked away from me.

"What kind of job?" I don't consider the possibility that she won't tell me until she presses her lips together. I'm hanging on for the answer, hoping the information will fill part of the hole she left.

A car door opens behind me and since it's either one of our daughters or Helena, I bite back my shout to leave me the hell alone. I haven't had a moment alone with Natalie since I moved out.

"Simon, we need to get going to catch the plane."

I hold my hand up to let Helena know I heard, but don't take my eyes off my wife—my *ex*-wife. "Look, Natalie. Remember Hayes's best friend, Brody Waite? He's been relentless about buying controlling shares of companies I'm looking to invest in, and when I called him to discuss why, he said he'd only talk to me if I could fly out."

Of course she knew who I was talking about. She knew about my brother's ex best friend and how Hayes had slept with Brody's now ex-wife. My brother was gone, so why was there a professional vendetta against me?

Natalie's pretty lips turn down. "Do you think he really can push you out?"

My gaze is caught on her mouth, but I nod. "One or two companies won't break us, but more than that could be serious. I need to know why he has me in his sights. He's too savvy of a businessman to let a grudge affect his decisions."

She rolls her lips in, her gaze darkening as it lands on the car. She isn't jealous of Helena, is she? I know my assistant is considered quite attractive. But Helena's married and I figure I should wait to date until I quit fantasizing about my ex-wife when I jack off in the shower. Whenever I do choose to date, I'll sure as hell stay away from my employees.

I only have two. I was about to hire more and expand when Natalie slapped the papers on my desk. It took two people to replace her, but it gave me something else to think about when my personal life was crumbling away.

If she's jealous, what does it mean? Every time she's around me, she's cool to the point of being a polar vortex.

"Fine. You can leave them with me."

I could stand here and gaze at her flushed face all day. But the plane is waiting. I wave the girls out. "Come out and give me hugs."

The goodbyes are quick. They already went through the disappointment phase, asking me why and when they could stay with me again. It can't be helped. If I want to leave them a legacy like my brother left me, I have to get to New York.

Natalie holds Maddy's hand and starts for the building, Abby next to her.

I don't know what possesses me, but I call out, "Oh, and Natalie?"

She stops and looks over her shoulder, her expression blank, as if she has better things to do in life than respond to me. It reminds me of how she'd be deep into studying for her exams and I'd tried to cajole her into taking a break. She could never resist me, just like I could never resist getting under her skin.

I grin. "Don't forget to stretch."

Two

Simon

I face Brody Waite across a boardroom table with downtown Chicago as the impressive backdrop behind him. The skyscraper office doesn't intimidate me. The private plane he sent for us, with its strict time lines, doesn't intimidate me. Not even the stern man sitting across from me wearing a watch that cost more than my suit intimidates me.

The glare Natalie shot me after I reminded her to stretch did the trick. How long has it been since she's been that fired up? Even our divorce was all stoic expressions and measured voices. She said she was miserable and I wanted to do what I could to mitigate her misery.

Even more, I wanted to do what I could to mitigate *my* misery. Having my wife tell me she was miserable and that it was my fault wasn't my best moment. I was reeling from shock when the papers were thrust in front of me. All I could think about was how, this time, I not only failed to meet my family's expectations—or lived up to them in this case?—but I failed my wife and kids and didn't know how. I was a mess inside and she was pulled together, professional, and had a fucking outline of how we'd co-parent.

But in that parking lot, she'd been hot, sweaty, and full of irritation. The gold in her blue eyes sparked—because of *me*. I didn't want to make her angry, but it was something, something other than her restrained appraisal when we exchanged the kids. It was filet mignon and wine to a starving man.

Brody interrupts my thoughts with an absurdly large number. Did I hear correctly? "Excuse me?"

"For Underwood Equity," Brody clarifies. "I'll buy you out."

My company is worth a lot. But not that much. It will be. It's heading in that direction and I won't stop until I surpass it. I built it from the ground up. Underwood Equity is the company that I dreamed about in high school and worked toward in college. So what's Brody's interest in it? Why trot me out to fucking Chicago to jerk me around about my company?

"Why?" He didn't answer me the first time I asked but inquired about how I linked up with the companies he was busy buying shares in.

"Why not?" His arrogant tone reminds me of my brother.

"Because this is business, and your problem with my brother was personal."

He frowns. "You think this is because I hated your brother and therefore hate you?"

I nod. That's exactly what I think.

He leans back in his chair, his shrewd gaze on me. "Did you know that he had an affair with Kayla?"

"I didn't know she was engaged to you before they got together."

Brody's right eye twitched.

Hayes would tell me things were good and business was good. Not much else about his family or his former best friend. Once I moved halfway across the country to the frozen tundra of the Midwest, we didn't talk like we used to. I think he assumed I'd move to Chicago and follow in his exact footsteps.

"I also had no idea Shayla wasn't his." My niece wasn't my brother's kid. A shock to us all.

I had a hard enough time living in his shadow. I wasn't going to drag Natalie into a life of constant judgment. She and I needed a place of our own to start our business and our family.

Brody nods, a faraway look in his eyes. "I've been following you. Impressive. What you did and from where you did it."

As if North Dakota is on the moon. "As long as there's internet and aircraft, I could build Underwood Equity anywhere."

His brows lift. "But you moved from Pennsylvania to North Dakota?"

I give a noncommittal shrug. "It was a growing business center then and it's more so now. We're a quick flight from Minneapolis, and from there, we can go anywhere." But Natalie's parents moved to Fargo after us, so we didn't need to travel. For so long, we couldn't afford to travel.

"And you have kids?"

"Two daughters." I don't peg Brody as a get-to-know-you guy. What's with the questions?

"And you're divorced?"

I clench my jaw, fed up with his prying. He can ask about my work, but I can't see why someone like Brody Waite cares about my personal life.

Before I reply, he sits forward. "You don't have to

answer, of course. But I've seen it a lot. Business takes off, personal life crumbles. Maybe you want to think about selling. I thought I could help."

My personal life is none of his business and a phone call would've sufficed. "The company is as much Hayes's as it is mine."

"He helped you start it?"

"No." I can't bring myself to tell him the rest. Being out here, where Hayes got his start, talking to his best friend, made it feel like my next stop should be to hang out with my brother.

His eyes narrow slightly before they infuse with understanding. "I see. Well, I'll reconsider my interest in our mutual clients. But... don't forget about me if you ever think about selling."

Not on his life, but I give him a smile. "How old is Shayla now?"

He rises and stretches out his hand. "Oh, you know. Seven going on twenty-seven, but I'm assured that's normal."

I shake his hand and chuckle, but my mind conjures that last image of my own daughters. My chest squeezes at the image of Natalie walking away with them. I miss them. Part of me wants to tell her how much, but I don't care to add to her stress. "It certainly is."

We leave the boardroom. Helena is bent over her phone. She's always working. Looking up, her gaze drifts between me and Brody, nothing but professional competence in the blue depths. Her demeanor is half the reason I hired her. The last thing I need to worry about is an assistant who wants in my bed.

"Looks like we'll get home in a few hours," I tell her. I might even get home in time to pick up the girls so we don't miss our night together. I'll be less salty about the trip if I get to hang with my kids tonight.

Relief crosses her face, but it's quickly covered with a neutral expression. "Oh, that's great."

Brody calls a driver to take us back to the airport. I mentally run through what I can work on en route and what can wait until I return. We're crossing the Queensboro bridge when my phone buzzes.

Natalie. I rush to answer.

"Simon." A sob echoes over the line. "When are you back in town? Mom collapsed and I'm at the hospital with the girls."

* * *

Natalie

My back has a kink in it and despite Aleah—and Simon—reminding me, I never did stretch.

I barely got home and showered when Dad called. Mom fell down in the kitchen and hit her head. He was following the ambulance and I met him at the big hospital on the edge of town. I drove by it a million times while it was being built after we first moved. I didn't think that I'd be sitting here one day, in a finished waiting room, worrying about my own loved one.

Mom's in ICU, and it guts me not to be with her, but an ICU room isn't where grandkids need to hang out with their grandma. We've been in the square waiting area for hours. They're tired of games on the tablet, the TV's playing "boring adult shows," and we've already unofficially toured the hospital twice.

"I'm bored," Maddy whines. This isn't the first time, but I can't blame her.

"Me too," I sigh. Abby's leaning over her chair to drape across me. I should take us all home, but I can't leave my mother's side, even if we're relegated to the waiting area.

I rest my head against the wall, debating on taking another cafeteria trip, when Maddy jumps out of her chair. "Daddy!"

Simon rushes in, looking the same as I saw him this morning. He's been wearing that suit all day with nary a wrinkle in sight. For what it cost, it should iron itself, but still. How can he look impeccable? I have on jean capris and a pink Under Armour T-shirt, and I look like both me and the clothes sat in the dryer for a few days.

He swoops Maddy up and I swear my ovaries have no idea how mentally exhausted I am because they implode. Abby runs to him as if she didn't just see him this morning. I want to do nothing but fall into his strong arms. I remain seated but can't fight my relieved smile.

"Hey, Mads." He gives Maddy a kiss, then Abby. His voice is the balm my frayed nerves need. "How's Nana?"

"She fell and hit her head," Maddy answers with the authority of an ICU doctor.

He looks at me and his brows furrow. "I thought she collapsed."

"I guess she's been fighting pneumonia and not taking it easy. She got light-headed and lost her balance. Her head hit the floor." Did my voice sound as tired as I must look?

He winces and sits beside me, turning Maddy to sit on a knee. "Did you know she was sick?"

"She told me she wasn't feeling well. But you know them. They *forget* to tell me about their health scares."

"You mean like when your dad didn't tell you that he had a hunk of skin cancer carved out of his forehead?"

"Exactly." We share a quick smile, but I rip my gaze away. It's too familiar. Makes me want too much. "So, your trip was fast."

"I don't get what Brody was playing at, but I got him to back off."

"Just like that?"

His face clouds over, but his anger quickly evaporates. "I think it was his way of testing me, vetting me as Hayes's namesake. As if I wouldn't make sure that my brother would be proud of what I'd built."

What *we* built. I'd thought of the company as a joint venture. Until it was clear it wasn't. Simon had too much to prove to everyone else, taking on so much work himself until I was relegated to various assistant duties.

"His way of forgiving his former friend?" I ask quietly.

"Something like that." He bounces Maddy on his leg and she giggles. Abby used to love it too. Does he realize he hardly ever sits with them like he's doing now? "It's behind me. Anyway, I tried to call my mom to see if they could come out, but she and Dad are touring Europe for the month."

As if his parents would lift a finger to help me. They might offer to take the girls on a world tour, but not if it benefited me at all. I don't expect an offer from that end. They'll stay away and hold out hope that Simon finds someone worthy of *them*.

"Do they ever get to see…" We don't talk much about it around our girls. Living over six hundred miles apart makes it hard to get close to their only cousin. Abby's old enough to remember her cousin Shayla and old enough to ask why she doesn't get to see her at all anymore.

"Once in a while. Not like before."

We're separated by armrests, but I'm tempted to lean into him. To let my head drop on his shoulder. Then he'd put his arm around me, tell me it'll all be all right, and I would believe him. Because he's Simon.

But I don't. "Do you mind if I go in Mom's room now? I'd like to sit with Dad for a while before they kick us out."

"Give me a call in the morning. I'll just go back to my plan of working from home for a day or two."

I don't know what possesses me to say the next words. He's offering to work from home. He says it like it's not a big deal, but it's huge. He hasn't missed going in to work for years. He didn't even make it a day during the week he was supposed to work from home with the kids.

But my impulsive idea makes sense. Really.

Except it could undo months of moving forward and rediscovering myself. "Why don't you just stay at the house tonight? I didn't get a chance to pack the girls' stuff."

I swallow hard and wait for his answer. I'm an adult. I can make this offer and not let it get my hopes up. Likewise, if he declines, I can acknowledge that it doesn't work for him and the reason is none of my business.

The way his jaw tightens as he slides his gaze toward me sends butterflies tumbling through my belly. I can do this. He would be a guest. The girls' father. Staying in the house we had big dreams for. The house we thought we'd entertain our grandkids in—together.

The offer is logical and not for my benefit. Not even for his. While he has a room for the girls and clothing at his place, he doesn't have Maddy's Pink Kitty, the stuffed cat with one eye, or Abby's Flipper, the stuffed turtle from the Fargo Zoo. Those are more critical to the kids than clothing.

"As long as you're okay with that," he says, his voice a low rumble, like he thinks it might mess with him too.

No getting my hopes up. It's just one night. Two at the most. The cold, emotionless man who had sat across the table from me, scribbling his signature on the divorce papers, wouldn't look at my offer as more than pure logistics.

I nod before I have the guts to say no. Doubts unfurl in my brain. Is asking him to stay at the house cowardly? Is it a sign that I can't let go when I really should? We were married eight years. Two months of separation and seven months of divorce aren't enough to get over that, but I can still be an adult.

The girls jump up and down and hug me. I break away. Simon still has a house key. He doesn't need more instructions from me, and I'm afraid to witness that the idea of sleeping under the same roof again doesn't affect him.

I'm not supposed to get my hopes up, but the thought that gives me strength as I walk to Mom's hospital room is that Simon is coming home.

Three

Simon

I wake up with Abby sprawled on the bed beside me and Maddy pressed into my back like she's determined to steamroll me off the bed. Good thing it's still ingrained in me to sleep in a T-shirt and shorts and that I had a small overnight bag with me in case I had to stay in New York.

I ease myself away from her and swing my legs down. Rubbing my eyes, I finish waking up while listening for Natalie.

Nothing.

I stagger out of the upstairs guest bedroom to the bathroom the room shares with the girls' bedroom. The guest room was supposed to be Abby's, but they wanted to be roommates. I could've used one of the two spare bedrooms in the basement that the girls are too afraid to move into but hated to be far from them when it's just us in the house.

And it'd feel too much like I was nothing more than a guest.

A shower will help me feel human. I forgot what a crappy night's sleep I often get living under the same roof as the girls. Between storms, growing pains, and just because, having one or both in bed with me is a common occurrence.

Does Natalie go through the day like a zombie? How easily I'd fallen into assuming that they'd outgrown it when I knew better. At my place, they share a bed and that helps more than sharing a room.

I yawn and flip on the light in the bathroom. Then I flip it back off. Natalie didn't mention that she wasn't the only one showering when she got called about her mom. The girls must've been taking one of their hurricane baths. Water had been drained out of the tub, but it was littered with toys, and clothing and towels covered the floor.

I go downstairs and across the house to the master bedroom, not bothering with the bathroom in the basement. If Natalie's sleeping, I'll suck it up and pick up the upstairs bathroom instead of letting her think she has another shower to clean downstairs.

The bedroom door is cracked open like normal. Well, *my* normal. From when I lived here. Walking through this house is so familiar it makes my fucking chest ache.

I push the thought away and peek inside. The bed's not made, but I was the bedmaker in the relationship.

She didn't come home.

I enter and shut the door behind me. As it clicks closed, the master bathroom door swings open and a very naked Natalie walks out with a towel wrapped around her head.

Too stunned to say anything, I stare. I can't look away and I know I should. I have to. This is a violation of her privacy. But good God, she's gloriously naked, and my eyesight sharpens like a hawk's. The droplets of water spattered on her shoulders are demanding to be licked off. I've always enjoyed the curve of her back, but new muscles ripple under her soft skin. And those breasts that I *know* fit perfectly in my hands are gently swaying, mesmerizing.

She looks over and yelps, the sound reminding me to spin around. Bare feet slap on the bathroom floor and the cabinet door opens. She's going to cover that sinful body.

What a shame.

"Sorry. God, I'm so sorry. I, uh..." I'm not though. I'm not sorry at all. I'm a thirsty man who's been stuck in the desert with nothing but saltines for six months and she's a single, perfect glass of water.

The faint stretch marks around her hips? I know which ones she got from Abby and the ones she blamed on Maddy. They've faded to whitish silver, but she'd gotten them growing *my* babies. Putting me in a suit doesn't erase my primal side.

"What are you doing in here?" She sounds calmer than she has a right to.

I would hold my hands up and turn around, but then she'll see what she did to me. Normally, I wouldn't care. But the last thing she probably wants is me tenting my shorts after I walked in on her—accidentally or not.

"The other bathroom was a mess, so I thought I'd cheat and shower in here."

Her sigh's unmistakable. She's tired. "That's right. I'll go clean it."

"No." I'm finally taking command of my erection. Her exhausted sigh did it. "I'll get it. I'm definitely awake now." I don't move though. I'm back in the bedroom with my wife. Leaving was hard the first time and I don't want to do it again. I have a question that's the perfect delay. "Are you going to the hospital again?"

"Not yet. The doctors do rounds in the morning. I'll relieve Dad before lunch. I wanted to get some of my training done."

Training? "Oh, for your job."

"Yes. It's all online."

"What kind of job?" She didn't answer me before and she isn't likely to while she's wrapped in only a towel. But I hope she does.

"You can turn around, you know."

I look up at the door and will her to drop the towel and invite me into bed and we'll forget this whole divorce mess. But when I turn around, my hopes crash. She's wrapped in a fluffy, deep-blue robe that covers her from neck to chin. She's adorable, but she showed more skin in her athletic clothes.

She twiddles her fingers when she answers. "I'm learning how to be a virtual assistant."

"A virtual assistant?" I echo. I thought being my assistant was part of what drove her away.

She nods, shifting her feet. Her toenails are painted a mixture of red, yellow, and blue on each foot. Pedicure day with the girls. "I know a lot already, but I'm brushing up on the business side and learning the social media platforms that I'm not really active in. I hope to launch after the Fourth of July. I figure harried working parents will be desperate for an extra hand around the beginning of school."

"Won't you be one of them?"

"It won't be as bad if I can work from home." She sits on the bed. No invite is extended to me and that damn robe manages to stay closed.

"Do you need more money from me?" I ask gently.

Hurt flashes through her face, followed by indignation. "And I would do what all day? Redo my nails and walk the rounds at the mall with all the retirees? I need something for *me*. What happens when I turn sixty-five and I have a retirement fund that I didn't start until I was in my forties?"

I assumed she would… no, that's a lie. I didn't think about her doing anything. She helped me, but ultimately, she was a stay-at-home mom. Only now, both of our kids will be in school. "Working for yourself, huh?"

"The best kind of boss."

She would be an amazing boss. There are still times I wish Helena or my personal assistant had Natalie's way with some of our clients. Helena doesn't take any special interest in their personal lives, but Natalie made sure to send baby gifts or condolence cards. And I don't know what happened between Charlie and the dry cleaner, but we had to make a switch and write off an entire suit.

"If you need any help…"

"I need to do this by myself." She inhales and squares her shoulders. "It's good for the girls to see me work for myself."

"Seeing you work for me wasn't good?"

Her voice is rigid. "Seeing me do nothing but work for you wasn't good."

"You weren't work—"

"Not that I *made* work for you, but that I was nothing more than a stapler or a folder or"—she flings a hand out—"a laptop."

I stare at her. Her cheeks are tinged with pink and it's nice and clear because the towel has her usually wild hair all wrapped up.

"I didn't realize you felt that way," I say stiffly.

She rubs her face with one hand, fatigue weighing her shoulders down. "All those times I asked you to take a break, to completely unplug so we could go on a real vacation, the hints about missing supper—again. But it was always about work until I didn't think you knew there was a difference between a wife and an assistant."

I jerk, her words hitting hard and unexpected. "How can you say that? I was—"

She cuts a hand through the air. "You know what? We're rehashing a marriage that's ended and I need to do some work before I go to the hospital."

"Fine." I hope the girls are still asleep. My expression has to look thunderous. Natalie's right about one thing—this isn't the time. But I have one thought as I take the stairs up to the other bathroom. *This isn't the end.*

* * *

Natalie

"Hi, Aleah. There's been a family emergency and I won't be able to meet you this week." I wince at how guilty I sound. But missing my appointments with my trainer makes me less guilty than ditching Dad at the hospital for a few hours.

"Oh no. I'm sorry to hear that. I hope everything's okay."

"I think it will be. My mom's in the hospital with pneumonia, so I'm taking turns with my dad staying with her."

"How are the girls doing?"

"Weird thing. Their father's actually jumping in to keep an eye on them."

"Mr. North Dakota?"

I nod, knowing that she can't see me. "In the flesh. Want an autograph?"

She laughs and I drop my head into my hands. Am I reading too much into the way his gaze devoured me when he caught me wearing nothing but a towel on my head? I know that look. If we were still married, I would've been flat on my back with my legs wrapped around him.

My body flushes hot, but it's not welcome. I never thought I'd feel this way again. I thought I'd moved on from the way he made me feel. Assumed that he didn't find me sexy anymore and that the divorce contract opened his eyes to the fact that he could get way more sophisticated and sexy women than me.

"No autograph necessary. Just your smiling face when you come back. I'll adjust your half-marathon training to account for the time off."

"Oh. Yeah. Thanks." I haven't thought of the race once since Simon stepped foot in the house. Between prepping for my online work and Mom, I can't think about fitting in runs, and I'm in the early stages of training. If a mile or two four mornings a week seems onerous, what's it going to be like when I'm up to six or seven?

As if she reads my mind, she says, "Don't worry about it. The point of the half is to challenge you and show you that you can do it. Life isn't going to stop because you want to train. We fit training around life. All I need you to do is drink water and get some rest."

"Water and rest. I can do that." I don't know if I can do that. I'm going to lie in bed worrying about Mom, fretting about starting my own business, and if I manage to drift off after that, the image of Simon gawking at me will keep me awake.

The call ends. I drop my phone on the bedside table and stare at the closet. I need to finish getting dressed. After Simon stormed out, I rushed to get a bra and underwear on, but I've been slumped on my bed since. The wet towel from my hair is on the floor. I'd get after the girls for that, but I can't bring myself to pick it up yet.

I didn't realize you felt that way.

He also doesn't realize that's the crux of the problem.

We were such good communicators and then he just... quit listening.

A knock at the door startles me. I jerk a sheet over myself. I didn't lock the door, dammit.

"Mom," Abby calls. "Can we watch TV?"

I nearly answer before I recall that Simon's here to be with them. "Ask your dad."

Footsteps scurry away and I hear Simon get bombarded with requests for TV and breakfast in front of the TV. A smile touches my lips. Abby's quick to capitalize on her dad's presence. There's no food allowed on the carpets and she knows it.

His deep voice filters into the bedroom. I can't make out the words, but the vibrations course through my body. He has a nice voice. Deep and resonant. I close my eyes and listen.

Shaking myself, I dart for the closet and dress in jean shorts and a T-shirt. I pack a tote with books and a tablet—both paper and electronic.

My hair is all over the place, as usual. I tame it into a braid and my shoulders are aching by the time I'm done. I drop my arms and stare in the mirror. My traitorous mind superimposes the image of Simon behind me, his fingers working through my hair.

"Then I do what again?"

I giggle. "Grab another hunk and cross it over between the fingers of your left hand." My scalp pinches as he tries to tug the curls free. "Ouch."

"I'm so sorry, babe. I need to quit."

"No. You can do it. You're good with your hands."

His heated stare meets mine in the mirror. "You know it."

And he did. He braided my hair until after Maddy was born and life got too busy. I'd sit between his legs in bed and he'd comb and tame the locks into a thick braid.

God, I missed my husband.

I spin on my heel and walk out. "Girls, I'm taking off."

"Mom." Maddy skids around the corner in her pink-and-white nightgown. Her hair is bunched up behind her head and I feel sorry for the comb that has to deal with that. She doesn't take getting her hair brushed well, but she's too young to do it well herself. "I have a picture for Nana."

She hands over a sheet of paper with two stick figures on it. I can only assume they're my parents. "She'll love it. Thanks, honey."

Abby comes over for a hug and I purposely keep my back toward the kitchen where Simon's clunking bowls and spoons around.

"Tell Nana we wish her the best." Simon ignores how I'm ignoring him. "And we'll visit as soon as she's ready."

I look over my shoulder. He's looming over the island with two bowls and two glasses. My heart tugs. He's making breakfast for the girls. It's only cereal, but it's enough to remind me of the husband I lost when his brother died three years ago.

I give the girls one last hug. "I'll give her big kisses from you all." Before I head toward the door, I hitch the tote over my shoulder and steel myself to look at Simon again. "Thank you."

He comes around the island and holds out a ziplock bag with a wrap inside. "A Nutella and banana wrap. You didn't eat breakfast, right?"

"Right." I planned to grab a bite at the cafeteria on my way to Mom's room. Or just go hungry until I traded out with Dad, which was the more likely scenario. Once I got to the hospital, I'd be too antsy to swing through the cafeteria and wait in line.

He hands over a bottle that I didn't notice before. "OJ."

I nod numbly and stumble toward the door to the

garage with my load in my arms. He made me breakfast. A wrap takes less than five minutes, but the thought behind it speaks volumes.

I spent months before our divorce missing my husband and he was under the same roof.

I have to keep reminding myself that this guy is only the aftereffects of Simon, like the tremors after an earthquake. Our marriage is over, but my world still needs to settle. Simon's here, but he's not my husband. A fault line cracked open and we're living on separate sides.

Simon

"Dad, look at the picture I drew."

I'm hunched over the desk in the office of my house—of *Natalie's* house. My place is a condo. A two-bedroom on the edge of downtown Fargo. It's the perfect pad for a corporate climber who prefers minimal maintenance and easy access to the trendiest after-hours spots in town.

I'm not that guy.

I'm a house guy. I like cutting the lawn and soaking up the smell of freshly cut grass. I like seeing my kids run and play with their shoes off and cartwheel over a carpet of grass. I like hearing rain on the roof and checking my basement for water after a heavy downpour.

I like talking to my neighbors when they walk by. Or stopping on my jog to catch up with Jake Miller and invite him and his wife and kids over. I like blowing out my driveway after a snowstorm and buzzing a path down the sidewalk to help dig the neighbor out.

I don't get any of that in my downtown condo. But, hey, it's close to my office.

I got a lot more work done there than I am in the home office. I've been interrupted to look at a stick figure holding flowers, begged to play a matching game, told to "come quick, Daddy" to see the garbage truck lift our canister to be dumped. Natalie's the one who remembered to set it out.

I have a housekeeper that my personal assistant arranges. I don't take my own garbage out anymore.

The picture I'm presented with this time is a portrait of me. Solid yellow for the hair and the face is square. "It's nice, honey. Now go watch a show. I've got to get some work done."

"I'm bored." Maddy twirls around and knocks down the paper shredder.

I dive for it, sending my chair into the wall. That'll leave a mark. I right the shredder and grimace at the pile of paper bits that poured out. How quickly I forgot the constant cleaning kids come with. I'm supposed to be easing Natalie's burden so she can be there for her mother, not leaving more work for her to do when she gets home.

"Give me a few minutes to make a call and then we'll go to a park." Never mind there's practically a full-service park in the backyard. A play set that includes a slide, monkey bars, and a covered sandbox. And if they played here, I wouldn't have to worry about what kind of condition the public toilets are in since they can't seem to go potty without touching the entire surface of the toilet.

My delay tactic works. She runs out and I call Helena. I haven't spoken to her since we landed. She needs to know the change in my schedule and that I won't get to everything on my calendar for the next day or two.

When she answers, I skip the usual chitchat I might've done with someone else, which Helena seems to have no interest in and begin with my instructions. "Listen, Helena, I need a few days for a family emergency. Can you reschedule my meetings this afternoon and all of tomorrow?" Natalie's words from when she told me she wanted a divorce come back to me. *You do nothing but work. You don't allow yourself a break and our family is suffering because of it.* "You know what—reschedule the whole week."

I'll show Natalie that I can take a fucking break.

"Mr. Underwood—"

"I know that'll mean overtime for you, but Natalie's mom is in the ICU."

There's a short pause, but Helena replies with a clipped, "Yes. Sure."

It's enough of a change from her normal response to make me notice. "Is everything all right? Did Milton call, irate about the shares I sold again?"

"No, Mr. Underwood. Everything's fine." She sounds more formal than usual. Everything's not fine, but I can't force it out of her.

"Great. I'll have my phone on me if there's an emergency." I hang up and look around the office that once used to be mine.

When we were just starting after college, newlyweds with a baby, Natalie used to bring Abby to the office. The same one I have now, much to my parents' dismay. They think I should have an entire office building to myself with a giant placard blaring my name in an eight-foot font. I'm getting there. It's only been three years since Hayes's death. The money he left me allowed me to finally gain footing in the industry. Growing beyond that and doing it the right way takes time. Takes competent people and the most competent one walked out of my life.

I've been meaning to hire someone new. Helena's been with me for over six months and could probably use an assistant of her own. Hell, Helena could probably become an adviser herself and we'd each need a new assistant. Then I would have to get someone who can do the office work and I'd be up to five employees, including me.

It just takes time. I'm already stretched as thin as I can go.

My gaze lands on an aloe plant in the corner, then skims over the walls decorated with pictures of our kids. This room had been pretty barren when I used it.

I stare out the window at the monstrous swing set. This house was the biggest purchase of my life, thanks to Hayes. We didn't grow up obnoxiously wealthy, but our parents insisted we put on a good show. That included a mortgage that stretched the budget until it screamed. Dad worked sixteen-hour days until he retired. Mom talked about her job like it was volunteer work, but it was a paid position, unlike the wives of the men in my father's social circle who upheld a very old-school mindset, one I never agreed with.

Hayes followed in Dad's footsteps but seemed to balance family life better than either of our parents ever did. Just like I failed to reach the status my brother did by my age, I failed at achieving that balance. I'm divorced and not living in the house I was able to buy without loans.

Dad pointed out that I should've funneled the house money into my business. Maybe I'd be further professionally and wouldn't have signed over a million-dollar house to my ex.

This place was way more house than Natalie and I needed at the time, but we talked about having four kids and figured it'd be best to have space for when they were older since we were in the unique position to choose. We wanted it to be the house that drew our kids back together when they were older and a place for the grandkids to congregate and get spoiled rotten.

Abby was starting preschool and Maddy was a baby when we'd bought this. Maddy's five now. Our family didn't grow to fill the house, but I don't regret the decision to move in. The girls have neighbor kids to play with and go to a nice school.

Did Natalie make an unconscious decision to stop having kids? Or had I missed those conversation subtleties too? We'd wanted to wait a couple years after Maddy was born before we tried again. Natalie had gotten pregnant on the pill before, so she stayed on it, and if it happened again, then we joked that it was fate.

Those couple of years were over a few years ago and we didn't even talk about it. I didn't think to bring it up. Did she?

I glower at the top of the desk while I ponder whether those questions are something I need answers to or if they're on a boat that's rowed out of my sight and none of my damn business anymore. I'm afraid of the answer.

She was an only child with a few cousins to play with growing up. I had my brother and couldn't imagine not having that sibling connection—at the time. I can imagine it all too well now. But growing up? We wrestled until we broke Mom's favorite vase. Then we snuck out and covered for each other. Hayes's gone, but our dad doesn't know that his pickup wasn't totaled by a hit-and-run when we were in high school. It was Hayes driving his friend's car—before Hayes had a license. The friend parked his vehicle in front of his house and let his own parents think it was a hit-and-run too. It's something we could laugh about as adults, but he's gone and I'll take that secret to the grave because he's my brother.

I scrub my hand down my face. I have a week off. Not really, but I'm available to help Natalie and will be around for my girls. I can even make dinner. I can grill. Natalie loved grilling season.

It might help distract her from realizing that I plan to stay here all week.

* * *

Natalie

I pull into the garage. Today was the longest day of my life. It doesn't feel like yesterday that I ran with Aleah. It seems like last week.

I almost punch the button in the car to close the garage door but stop. It's garbage day. I need to bring the bin back.

I frown. I can't recall seeing it when I drove in. But I took it to the curb this morning before I went to the hospital.

What I had passed driving into the garage was Simon's Mercedes. His car was parked there all night. How many of the neighbors noticed?

Do I have to ask? All of them.

Did he bring the bin in?

I can count on one hand the number of times he's done that. A small chore but one he had to be home to do.

I even did the lawn care for the last couple of years until I had to throw in the towel and hire a service. Keeping the girls contained so I could ride around on the John Deere was too big of a challenge. And Simon was always working. Now they're old enough to play while I mow, but I keep the lawn service because I can. The same goes for snow removal and I even hired a maid service that comes once a month. Because if I did all of that shit, I'd be reminded that the dream house Simon and I purchased is way too damn big for a single mom.

I walk to the garage door opening and peer out. There it is. The bin. Put back in its place.

Sucking in a breath, I blow it back out. It's nothing. One two-minute chore doesn't mean he's a changed man. And if he has changed, it doesn't mean he wants me back.

With that thought, I spin on my heel and go inside. The girls' faint laughter filters through the house. Closing my eyes, I soak it in. After a day spent by Mom's bed, I need this. I need to come home and just have it all already dealt with.

I see Simon out on the patio through the blinds of the French doors next to the kitchen. The girls are frolicking in the sprinklers. The smell of steaks grilling hits me and my stomach rumbles. The cafeteria sandwich I ate for lunch was hours ago.

I step outside and get my first look at Simon. My mouth drops open. He has athletic shoes on—and it isn't just for his morning run. Not only that, but he's wearing navy shorts and a striped button-down linen shirt. Casual Simon hasn't made an appearance for years.

He looks over his shoulder and lifts his chin. "Hey, how's your mom?"

"Janie Wagner will live to see another day, if only so I can kill her for not going to the doctor sooner." I flop into a lawn chair. The girls squeal and wave at me as they take turns on a Slip 'N Slide.

We don't have a Slip 'N Slide.

"Did you go to the store?" Does he even remember where they are? His personal assistant sees to all his meals.

"Yeah, wow, they really redid Target. So your mom didn't go to the doctor? But I thought you knew she had pneumonia?"

"She wasn't getting better despite being on meds and ignored it. They've switched her antibiotic and have her on breathing treatments. The head issue wasn't serious, thank God."

"She'll pull through okay?"

"They're going to keep her another day or two to make sure it's all working, then they'll cut her loose. But she'll be in a regular room so the girls can go see her. I said we'd be by tomorrow. I'll have to have a serious talk with them. When I go help Mom out after she's released, she's going to be so worn out. They can't expect her to be an active grandma for a few weeks."

"Leave them with me." He shrugs. "I took the week off. Helena's taking charge. I'll get her to cover the evening calls and meetings too. Our London investors are pretty quiet in the summer."

"Doesn't Helena have a life?" And how much does Simon participate in it? I bite back the thought. I hate petty jealousy. Besides, he's a single man. *Eligible.* I should concentrate on his declaration that he's taking a week off, but it's a case of *I'll believe it when I see it.*

"I have no idea, but she doesn't say anything."

"Why would she? You're the boss." Ironically, I'm not too jealous to advocate for her. I know what working for Simon is like.

His expression darkens. "I'm not a bastard."

"No, but you're pretty oblivious to the personal lives of others."

He waves the metal spatula around like a wand. "If she needs time off, she'll say so."

He can go ahead and think that. It's not my job anymore. "So what'd you guys do all day?"

"The park, the store, and then I promised them

hamburgers, but I got you and I rib eyes. And I guess we're watching *Frozen*."

"It's cute. I've seen it ten times."

"So you aren't going to join us?" He makes it sound casual and it feels a lot like when he asked me on our first date.

I thought instead of the party the guys were going to throw, I'd catch a movie if you wanted to come with me.

I'd gone back to my dorm and jumped up and down with my roommates. The frat boy stud asked me, studious uncool girl, out. The rest is history, just like our marriage.

"No. I'll take advantage of you staying here to catch up on some training."

He nods, but disappointment simmers in his eyes. He wants to hang out with me? He's actually taking time off and he wants to spend it with me. That's a revelation I don't need to look deeper at.

If I go ahead and snuggle up in the recliner to watch the movie, I'll start to remember how good it can be between us. How nice it is to have us all together.

Then he'll go back to work and crush those fantasies. If he's going to be here all week, then I'll have to concentrate on what I've been letting slip when he can't hold up his end of the co-parenting gig. My half-marathon training. The business I'm starting.

I had big plans once. By the time I graduated with my college degree, I was pregnant and married. Not exactly the high-powered CEO I envisioned myself as. My professional dreams and having kids shouldn't be mutually exclusive. I can be a mom and a businesswoman. But those plans are the first to take a back seat when life gets busy. I'm not even thirty. Do I have to wait until I'm forty before I get my chance?

I've never discussed my issues with him. The few times I

brought them up shortly before the divorce, he circled the conversation back to Underwood Equity, insinuating that I had my chance.

Anyway, he has enough hang-ups with his family. He's proven unwilling to handle mine. Simon's presence makes it hard to concentrate, and it's him manning my grill that's bringing up all these questions I've been ruminating over for years.

"I'll head to the office. Let me know when dinner's ready." I don't bother to look at him. Instead of feeling prudent, the sense that I'm running from him follows on my heels.

Natalie

I drape Mom's bedspread over her. Dad and I had brought her home from the hospital and shuttled her straight to bed despite her protests that she was fine to sit in a chair. If we get her settled in her chair, she won't rest. She'll straighten the end table, and that would lead to a little dusting and maybe popping outside to check the garden.

"I've been doing nothing for days. I don't think I can rest any more."

Says my mom with the pale face, who ended up short of breath walking from the garage to the bedroom.

I put my hands on my hips. "You might not sleep, but you can rest. What do you need done?"

Mom purses lips that haven't returned to their normal deep pink. "After the rain earlier this week, the weeds are probably going wild."

"I'll weed before I go." Dad, with his bad back,

shouldn't be out in the garden trying to figure out what's crabgrass and what's sweet corn. "What else?"

"Oh, honey. I don't want to—"

"Simon's with the kids. I've got all day."

Mom falls quiet, her contemplative stare in no way diminished by her illness. "He's been helping quite a bit."

"Well, he always liked you." Being around Mom gives him a chance to witness a mother figure who gives a shit and doesn't cut him down every moment she gets.

"Is he staying at the house?" Her question's deceptively innocent as she straightens the blankets across her chest.

"Yes, actually. He didn't really ask and it's been so handy, I just…" I shrug. If it wasn't for Mom in the hospital, this would've been perfect, months too late, but perfect nonetheless.

"Uh-huh. Is he sleeping in the guest room or in your room?"

"Mom," I admonish, but my cheeks heat. She tries to laugh but breaks out in a junky cough.

Dad saunters in. "What's this about you and Simon?"

"*Nothing*. We're still divorced. But according to that article, he co-parents. I couldn't believe it at first, but that's what he's been doing all week."

Mom sighs and relaxes into her pillows. "I still remember the first time you told us about him, and I thought he'd be a pretentious young man. He kind of proved me right toward the end, but I think there's still hope for him."

"Don't hold out too much. He's on his phone whenever the girls are occupied and I heard him taking some conference calls in the middle of the night."

"I wish he'd get his head straight." Dad sets a glass of water on the bedside table.

I use it as an excuse to extract myself from this conversation. "Well, I'd better get out and weed. I have to stop at Target before I head home."

I tie my hair in a messy bun on the way to the backyard shed, unable to escape the sensation that this is too good to be true. Simon won't be around that long. The siren call of work and living up to his brother's legacy will lure him away.

But it hasn't yet and I'm free to help Mom. I find her gardening gloves and the rest of her supplies. Selecting a trowel and the claw tool, I head out to her coveted gardens. Evaluating the job and the way the weeds seem to mutate after a nice rain, I pick a side to start on.

Dad meets me in the garden with a hoe.

"I've got it, Dad. You have other things to do."

"I need some fresh air after being stuck in the hospital for so many days. And if I don't try to save these jalapeño plants, she won't be able to hand them out like candy at the church social this fall."

Mom's garden is more than a hobby. It's an obsession. She pickles and cans and everyone that passes her during preserving season gets a jar of something from the garden. I usually help her. I plan to help her this year, and I've started fortifying myself for the emotions it's going to bring up.

Last year was when I decided over a boiling pot of salsa that I couldn't do it anymore. The girls and I stayed overnight to help can applesauce and apple pie filling the next day, staying away the whole weekend—and Simon didn't notice. He pulled late nights at the office and used up all the individual freezer meals I made him. When we returned home, I had a full night of prepping him another week's worth of meals for the office, confirming my decision to look up a divorce lawyer the next day.

I rip out a weed. Then another and another until sweat drips down my face. Dad's white legs come into view. He hoed through the rhubarb and cleared around the larger and more obvious plants like the squash.

"Want to tell me what's really going on with you and Simon?"

I sit back on my heels and squint up at him. A chemical, woodsy smell rolls off him. Bug spray. I probably have mosquito bites all over.

The incessant itching will take my mind off other, much more dangerous feelings tonight in bed when my body is well aware that my ex is under the same roof. Maybe if he wasn't so good in bed, I would've left him sooner. Just another reason I can't trust myself around him.

"There's nothing to tell. He took off work and is carrying the weight around the house so I can help Mom. I'm even getting all caught up on my training so I can start my own business." Aleah, Rachel, and my parents are the only ones I've told about Let Me Assist You.

Simon was the last to know.

"That's awesome." Dad's look is the same one he got in high school when I ran the car out of way more gas than it took to get to the grocery store. "Then what?"

"Then he goes back to work and I start my own business."

"There's no chance that you two..."

"Nope. He's still married to the company." I wipe my forehead with the back of my wrist. The fingers of my gloves are black, but I'd need to garden for another eight hours before I ripped enough weeds to straighten out half my thoughts.

"Then you don't think he's started dating?"

"He works too much to meet anyone. I don't think he's involved with his assistant." I didn't plan to say that. I'm not aware of when I accepted that there's nothing with him and Helena, but he's too absorbed in his career.

"Isn't she married?"

"That doesn't always stop people."

Dad shrugs. "Simon never struck me as that kind of guy. Besides, if he was interested in doing, you know, *that*, he wouldn't have hired Charlie. I'm sure plenty of attractive young women applied."

"Charlie's still attractive."

"And not Simon's type."

I can't deny that I worried about who Simon would surround himself with at work. Not everyone applying to work with him would be interested solely in professional development. Simon's my age and when we were married, even during the times I was so frustrated with him I could hardly stand to look at him, I couldn't deny him in bed. He got what he wanted and he wanted it a lot. And no matter how conflicted my mind was about him, about us, my body never doubted how good, how cherished, he'd make me feel.

The thought that he'd move on and do that for someone else kept me awake too many nights over the last seven months.

"He hasn't changed." I'm done with this conversation. It doesn't help to know that my parents would support a reconciliation. "The company comes first. The company *always* comes first."

"Maybe when he goes back to work, he'll realize everything he's been missing."

"He's had seven months to do that." More if you counted when we separated those couple of months before the divorce was final.

I know Simon better than anyone. That's why I called the divorce attorney. Simon's single-minded. A handsome guy like him never quits getting hit on just because he wears a wedding ring. But he was focused on me. A heady experience for a girl who drifted through life never standing out.

The company came and it was our priority. Then, the girls got older and my priorities shifted. Hayes died and Simon's priorities shifted. I lost my husband. My partner.

His single-minded focus is growing that company to something his big brother would've boasted about at country clubs across the nation. Hayes's company was a whopping success and Simon's determined to outdo him ten times over.

I can't compete against a dead man.

* * *

Simon

I lie awake and stare at the ceiling. It's one of the few mornings I don't wake up with a kid in bed. Somehow, they remember in the dark of night that I'm across the hall and find me instead of trekking across the house to Natalie's bed.

It's also one of the few mornings I don't have a ton of messages from Helena. Apparently, Brody pulling out of the companies I invested with left my clients panicking that something was wrong with my choices. Helena's had her hands full the last few days. It wasn't like I could tell them that the guy hated my brother and was toying with me or something like that.

I still haven't figured it out.

I let out a long breath. The house is quiet, but I'm sure Natalie is in the office. Every night, I've gone to bed harder than I'd ever been. I have to lock myself in the shower and stealth jack off after bedtime. I switched to nighttime showers so I don't have to worry about the kids pounding on the door to ask for their eighth snack of the morning or yelling about a show they can't agree on.

Natalie spends her mornings in the office, listening to training courses and setting up her business. I want to ask her more about it, but she deflects me every time. I get the impression she assumes I'll think it's lame. I'm proud as hell of her.

I swing my legs down and rub my eyes. After getting dressed in black shorts and a white T-shirt, I go to the bathroom. I take an extra minute to finger-comb my hair after I brush my teeth. I should get a trim, but for once, it's nice to be casual from head to toe. I skip shaving. Again. My morning routine is shot to hell and that alone feels like more of a vacation than our trip to Niagara Falls for our honeymoon.

I head downstairs and tell myself to keep going to the kitchen and start breakfast, but I head straight for the office. Tapping lightly on the door, I don't hear anything. Taking a chance, I open it.

Natalie looks at me, then whips her head back to the computer screen, but not before I see her glistening eyes.

I cross to her and drop to my knees. "What's wrong?"

She sniffles and sighs, accepting that I caught her crying and I'm not leaving. "It's this—It's nothing."

"Natalie, you don't cry over nothing." She tears up at movies where the love story ends in a funeral. She cried when her grandparents died, and when she was pregnant, she cried at—well, I couldn't predict when it'd happen then, just a lot. But other than that, she holds her emotions in, only opening up to me when she really needs to talk.

That she's reluctant to let me in now is a kick to the nuts.

She waves at her computer. "This job. Am I crazy to think I

can do this? How do I even find my first client? I've been in this office for hours trying to figure it all out. I can't open my virtual doors and hear crickets. The girls are going to ask. They're going to ask how many people I'm working for and they're going to ask how the business is going. And what if... what if I suck?" A tear escapes each eye and streaks down her face.

I gently brush them away with my thumbs. "One, you don't suck. You know that. Two, you're going to kill it because you know how to do the job and you want it."

"I haven't done it virtually. This isn't like picking up dry cleaning and grabbing coffee."

"You did more than that." Underwood Equity was our brainchild. She might've done a lot of administrative duties, but only because she wanted to be free for the kids. I clasp her hands. "Whatever is asked of you, you'll be fine. You'll figure it out and you'll be good. Before you know it, you'll be so in demand that you'll have to turn clients away." She makes a face, but I press on. "Remember that statistic? The one that said women wait to apply for a job until they're like ninety percent qualified and men will apply even if they're ten percent qualified?"

She gives me a small smile, but it's a win. "I don't know if those percentages are correct."

"The point is, you're going to do great. You're going to be awesome." I look at my big hand over hers. "You were the best thing that happened to me."

She goes rigid. "Simon—"

"I mean it. I can't imagine anyone who'll be better at this job than you. You were excellent in the company and you did a hell of a lot more than pick up dry cleaning. You're an amazing mother. And you were the only wife I ever wanted."

More tears spill over. She rolls her lower lip in. "You were the only husband I ever wanted."

The question "Then why?" is on the tip of my tongue, but the last thing I want is the same old fight that'll drive more distance between us.

Instead, I show her how I feel. Her face is only a couple of inches higher than mine, where I'm kneeling on the floor.

I flatten my hands on her thighs and stretch up. Our lips press together and I don't force it. How's she going to react?

She doesn't at first. But she isn't pulling away. My body's shaking from the restraint. We haven't been apart nearly long enough for me to forget what it's like between us. If I wasn't captivated by her smile and the way she moves through life, then I would've been irrevocably tethered to her based on the chemistry between us.

I add pressure to her lips and hers melt under mine. *Finally*. She tastes of mint and tears and it's familiar from our years together.

She sighs and cups my face with her hands. Triumph races through my blood, but I hold myself still. This isn't about me. This is about offering comfort and support the only way I know how.

When she opens for me and our tongues touch, my fingers dig into her thighs. I relax my hands and stroke them up and down her legs.

I want this woman. I always have.

Her tongue clashes with mine and she scoots to the edge of the chair. I can wrap my arms all the way around her.

Blood rushes to my groin until I'm harder than I've been in months. The object of my fantasies is in front of me again.

Footsteps pound on the floor. "Mom? Dad?"

Natalie gasps and shoves against me. Her chair wheels back until it hits her desk. Her eyes are wide and her lips are pink from my kiss.

I sway but stay where I am. The situation won't get better with my erection on display.

"We're in here," I call over my shoulder.

Maddy appears at the door. I can't turn fully around without inspiring questions about the bulge in my shorts.

Natalie props her arm on the desk and sinks her head in her hand. "What's up, peanut?" she asks, all nonchalant.

Maddy hugs her stuffed cat. "I thought you were gone."

"Nope, we're here." Natalie's tone is bright and rings false. Our kiss bothers her. Logically, I know it's a complication, but I can't bring myself to care.

"Okay. Can I watch TV?"

"Only until Abby wakes up," I say. Otherwise, Maddy will bug Abby until she wakes up and an Abby that's short of sleep is like having a cranky bear cub around the house.

When Maddy pads away, I look at Natalie.

Her cheeks are red and her gaze is boring into her black computer screen. "That was a mistake."

"It doesn't feel like it."

Her brow crinkles and she meets my gaze. "We can't do that again. If the girls see, they'll think..."

"That I still care about you."

She scowls. "This divorce is hard enough."

"Is it?" When her gaze hardens, I continue. "Because it seemed so easy for you to leave. It was all planned out."

"It had to be. You had all the power. The business was in your name, and all the retirement was in your name."

"My name, but it was ours." And now half is mine and half is hers.

"I want to be my own person, Simon." Her voice is quiet. "That includes having a purpose of my own outside of what I do as a wife and mom. I need to be a good role model for the girls."

I understand what she's saying, but I don't. She never

said she felt like anything less, and I didn't think I treated her like that. Our life was busy.

"Natalie..."

"Simon. The girls can't see us and get excited that there's more here than there really is." Her jaw tightens and resolve fills her eyes.

If I want to make headway with her—and after that kiss, I *know* I do—I don't push it. "Okay. Finish up in here. I'll make breakfast."

I leave her alone in the office. My body might have calmed down, but my mind is spinning. I respect her wishes to keep the girls out of it. I don't want them hurt and confused any more than she does. But that doesn't mean I can't woo my wife under their radar.

Natalie

Simon took the whole week off.

Oh, I know he was on his phone whenever he could sneak away, but it's Saturday, and he was physically present the entire week. The girls are in daddy heaven.

But my mom's doing better and my dad sees through my excuses to escape the overpowering presence of my ex-husband.

"Kick him out or move him back in."

"It's not that easy, Dad."

Simon's not moving back in. Not when I've started feeling like an independent adult. But I can't bring myself to kick him out.

I'm hiding in the office. I've gone through all my training and even listened to a few entrepreneurial podcasts. My education wasn't long ago, but when I listen to all the new terms about financial independence and profit first, it feels like ages ago.

This was easier when I let Simon take the lead, which he did effortlessly. He works with as much confidence as he lives the rest of his life. His parents might be a high-maintenance mess, but they instilled in their kids the belief that there is nothing off-limits in the world.

"I can do this," I mutter under my breath as I shut my computer down. My next step is to write a detailed business plan now that I'm mostly trained and know what I can offer and the commitment required.

After that, well... then I have to start working the system I've been painstakingly planning.

When I leave the office, the rest of the house is quiet. Did they go outside?

I glance out the window. The sky is dark blue. Rain is on the way. I hope they didn't go for a walk, or if they did, that they'll be home soon.

Voices drift down the stairs.

Ah. The girls are in their room. Is Simon playing with them?

I jog up the stairs. His voice becomes clear. The door to the girls' bedroom is cracked open and both the girls are planted in front of their Barbie dream house. Simon must be on the phone in the guest room.

I don't mean to spy, but I step closer to the guest room door and hear him say, "I'll probably be back in the office on Monday. Why don't you take the call and send me a report?"

My mouth twists. He doesn't see the irony in wanting to take a weekend while making his assistant do it. When I worked with him, I quit asking the question, "But does this need to be done on the weekend in the first place?"

Simon didn't realize that some of his clients were divorced workaholics who were alone in life and if he didn't set limits, he'd end up the same way. And look what happened.

Except he's clearly taking the weekend off and sloughing the duties off onto Helena.

But it's not any of my business anymore.

"Thanks," he says. "And can you return Lancaster's call? I forwarded the email to you already."

Helena probably has a full workday ahead of her.

I must've made enough noise to catch the girls' attention. "Mommy, are you done in the office?"

I lean against their doorframe. "Yes. But it looks like a rainy day. What should we do?"

Abby pivots away from the dollhouse, her legs twisting in a way that would land me on the couch for days, rehabbing a sore knee. "Daddy said we should go to the movies."

"Is there anything good out?"

Simon speaks behind me, making me jump. "There's always a kids' movie in the theaters, right?"

"I need to run." One, I'm not committing to a family outing. I'm too raw and it sounds too good. And two, I haven't done a thing to train all week. I don't want to show up to my next session with Aleah and be out of breath before we even finish our warm-up.

His eyes light up. "Underwood family workout?"

Abby cheers and jumps up. Confusion puffs Maddy's lower lip out. "What's that?"

She was still in diapers the last time we all hung out in the home gym together. Only in those days, Simon punished himself on the treadmill and I entertained the kids while half-assing some weights.

Abby grins and explains. "Daddy plays the music really loud and sings along while he's running and we're down there with him."

Simon's grin matches his daughter's. "Only this time,

Mom is going to be on the treadmill singing. Runner's choice."

A staggering case of self-consciousness hits me. This is worse than a family movie date. I've never run in front of Simon. Walked on the treadmill, yes. Walked outside, of course. Ran while he chased me with promises of tickling me silly, yes. But not, like, a real show of athleticism.

Running is something I do for an escape from the real world. To build myself up after the hurt he caused. I don't want to do that in front of him. If it wasn't too early, I'd suggest we go to the movies immediately.

Simon starts down the stairs. "Get your shoes on, girls. I'll grab the water bottles."

They're all crazy excited while I'm standing here dying inside because I don't want my ex-husband to drop in a fit of laughter over seeing me try to run for real. I can't fall apart on the treadmill and sob in front of my girls. That hasn't happened for months, but my wounds aren't fully healed.

But as I watch the girls race around their room, changing T-shirts because they think the new ones are better to work out in, it's clear they're second-guessing nothing. In their world, why wouldn't I do something as simple as running on a treadmill in front of them and their dad?

Be a good role model.

If I can do this, I can do the movies without my heart hurting so bad I can't sleep.

I swing by my bedroom and get changed. By the time I hit the basement, music is pumping from the speakers. Simon is running the kids through steps that look like a line dance we once learned in a college class.

I make my way to the treadmill as if I'm trudging through shin-deep snow. The song switches out to a fast-paced dance song. I glance at Simon. His back is to me, but he found my playlist as easily as he does everything else.

I warm up with a brisk walk that stretches longer than normal. Finally, I push the speed up. My feet hit the belt with a steady rhythm and I get lost in the sound of the motor and the music.

Until Simon appears at my side.

My right foot hits the outside edge of the belt and I steady myself on the arm rails.

"Sorry." He puts a hand on the outer edge of the treadmill monitor and his other hand on his hip. The girls are jumping over weights behind him. He made them a makeshift obstacle course. "So what made you pick up running?"

I gasp-talk to Aleah when I'm running. I have no intention of doing it in front of Simon. I punch the speed down until I'm walking. The distance is a mile shorter than intended, but at least I ran.

"I thought a half-marathon would be good for me and when I mentioned it to Aleah, she was so confident that it was possible."

His brows lift. "A half, huh?"

I nod. "I didn't think of it in time to do the Fargo Marathon, but there's a women's half in August. She thinks I'll be able to get my training in."

"Of course you can." He says it simply, like he's more assured than Aleah or Rachel, who had invited me over to watch the Fargo Marathon last month. The path went by her house and her kids loved to cheer on the racers. Watching sparked my ambition and Rachel told me to go for it. So did Aleah. Now Simon. Apparently, I'm the only one who lacks faith.

He's standing close and I'm hot and sweaty. There've been many times we were like this and I didn't care and we both ended up in the shower together. I have to get away from him. "You want to take a turn?"

"Sure, if you're done."

We switch places and I hang out with the kids, running through the course Simon made for them. The girls change the rules each time.

It's not long before I regret getting off the treadmill. Not because I'm not having fun but because I shouldn't be too insecure to run with my ex in the room. I should've owned it and finished what I planned to do.

I have a chance to when Simon hops off the treadmill. Sweat wicks down his shirt, but it doesn't stop him from rearranging the obstacle course, adding more weights for the girls to jump over. I stand with the girls, fascinated by how he's expanding it and increasing the difficulty.

He hands his phone to Abby. "I need you to time. I'm racing your mom."

My eyes go wide. "You're what?"

Jumping from foot to foot, he rolls his neck. "You and me. A race."

"I-I don't..." I was about to say race, but isn't that what I'm down here training for? I don't plan to race other runners, just myself. This is different. It's a downstairs, homemade obstacle course. I didn't finish my mileage. I can make up for chickening out by jumping over a few weight stacks. "Be ready to call *American Ninja Warrior* by the time I'm done."

Without waiting for Abby to start the clock, I take off. Simon's laugh bellows out of him and bounces off the walls. He claps and cheers and the girls join in as I round one of the curves in the winding course.

Before I'm done, he starts, whipping through each small challenge much faster than I was able to, closing in on me.

A squeal rips out of me and I add more speed, thrilling

adrenaline racing through my veins. At the next jump, the toe of my shoe catches the top weight. It slides and I lose my balance. My arms cartwheel and I hop on one foot when strong arms close around me and I'm pressed against a hard chest.

The gasping laugh that leaves me is from a different woman, a carefree one having the time of her life. Simon joins as he rights me, his chuckle vibrating next to my ear.

Taking his time, he releases me. Sweaty or not, I could've handled being in his arms a lot longer.

The girls cheer and rush us, cutting off any awkwardness after Simon's save. I give high fives to each of them, but when I lift my gaze to meet Simon's, my heart clambers into my throat and my body flushes with heat that has nothing to do with my recent exertion.

His eyes are hooded, his look knowing. If this was three years ago and the girls were in bed or at my parents, I know what'd happen next.

I avert my gaze and take the phone from Abby. I was bold enough to race Simon, but I'm back to being a chicken. Keeping my emotional distance from Simon is a lot easier when we're not touching—and when he doesn't have a chance to look at me like he wants to lick me clean.

"Who's racing Dad next?"

* * *

Simon

The weekend is almost over and I know if I leave here and go to work tomorrow, then it's all over. I'll go back to my condo when work's done and see the kids one night a week and every other weekend.

I glance over my computer at where the girls are playing on the lawn. The deck smells like citronella and we're all loaded with an obnoxious-smelling bug spray that claims to be natural. The coolness of a June morning is losing way to the summer sun with a dash of extra humidity from the rain we got yesterday.

But the girls are content and I can snatch a few moments to catch up with my inbox.

Natalie's on her way back from her parents. My mother-in-law is doing better but still weak. I can't take another week off and an unfamiliar feeling settles into the middle of my chest.

Resentment.

I want more time with my family. I need more time to win Natalie back. Why can't I get away for longer? If it wasn't for Helena, I wouldn't have gotten the week I did.

As it was, I still clocked plenty of time on my phone and on my laptop during the late-night hours.

I stuff the feeling away. I wouldn't have gotten this far without the money Hayes left behind. My company is relatively young and I have no business resenting the time it takes to make it successful. It's my legacy. It's going to be what I leave the girls, whether they go into investing or not. When they were born, Natalie and I barely had a quarter each to rub together.

In those days, I was terrified that something would happen to me. Natalie had her parents, but we couldn't count on mine. They had retirement funds they used to constantly travel the world and avoid their personal problems.

Natalie threw all her support and education behind me and Underwood Equity. I was frantic to build it to a stage where it could support her and our kids if something happened to me.

No one predicted my brother would have a heart attack and die behind the wheel. But he'd left enough to take care of his wife and the child and me.

I'm tackling the detailed reports Helena sent. I can do both—win my wife back and run a successful business. I'll make damn sure I get it done.

One of our top clients is trying to micromanage his accounts instead of trusting me to do my job. I don't mind fielding questions and inquiries, but when I can prove his investment ideas actively lose money, he doubles down. And it's usually on the weekend. I'm certain it's after he plays eighteen holes with his equally rich and bored friends, who I suspect get shitty investment advice from several people in their lives.

My phone lights up and I'm grateful for the distraction from the Lancaster mess. Sending Helena to deal with him should've been a no-brainer. Lancaster can be a pest because he misses the adrenaline of high-stakes business. We've become good friends over the years and he even had me and Natalie over to his place before he moved to Arizona. And that's probably why Helena can't get very far with him.

I answer and Charlie's chipper voice flows through the phone. "Sunday check-in, boss. Is this a good time?"

"It's fine."

"Great." He runs down the list that's the same every week. "So, your suits have been picked up and delivered to your place. The freezer is packed with heat-and-serve meals and I put a few in your fridge at the office in case you end up eating in." That happens more than I anticipated. Conference calls that drag on for hours. New company profiles to study. I have a dorm fridge and microwave in my office for such occasions. Most days, Charlie orders in for me and Helena. The meals in the fridge are for the evenings and weekends when no one's around to make the order.

"The maid service called last Wednesday. You had a leaky faucet. It's already been fixed."

Right. My place. How easily I've settled back into the house.

"Anything else you want to add for the upcoming week?" He asks the same each Sunday, and I never fail to have a short list. Today, I've got nothing.

"No. Sounds good, Charlie. Thank you."

"No problem, Mr. Underwood. I have my phone on me if you need anything."

I disconnect the call. When was the last time I saw Charlie in person? I hired him and we had in-person check-ins for a time, but once his proficiency was clear, I didn't feel the need to cross paths with him. He used to be skittish about open access to my place. But he realized that he wasn't going to walk in on me with anyone else, and now he comes and goes when he needs to. The only way I know he's been there is that my suits are gone and replaced by Monday.

I try to think about Lancaster, but my mind is mulling over how nice this weekend has been so far, with minimal disturbances. I've been getting some work done and have been taking calls, but I wake up with my kids, braid some hair, and get to spend the morning watching them play.

The sliding door opens and Natalie steps out. The wind ruffles the coppery curls around her face. She looks soft and approachable. It's instinct to get up and give her a kiss. We're not there—yet.

I keep my ass seated but close my laptop. Work for today is done. "How's your mom?"

"Better. She said she got through yesterday without napping. She might nap today but wants to get outside for some sun."

"That'll be good for her."

"As long as Dad can keep her out of the garden. She

needs to work up slowly and she won't once she puts gardening gloves on." She sits in the chair next to me. Her sunglasses are still on, hiding her expression.

"I can make sure I'm around this week."

Her brow crinkles over her shades. "Take another week off?"

She makes it sound like I announced we're sailing across the world. "No, but I can come over for a bit each evening so you can get some work done."

She stares at me. "Each evening?"

I shouldn't be so insulted by her disbelief. I need to prove that I can do it. I did it before when we were married.

Well, I usually brought the work home, which will happen again. But with Helena's help, I can carve out a few hours each night. A few hours that will be easier if I'm around. "Why don't I bring my supplies for the week over? That way, I don't have to waste time going back and forth."

Her mouth forms a troubled line. "I don't think that's a..."

"I'll be around in the mornings if you get up early or in the evenings." She's going to try to do it all herself. Whether it's her default or because she thinks I'll flake, I have to convince her to let me help. "You still need to check on your parents?"

"I can do that with the girls."

"Don't swimming lessons start this week?" I don't miss the look of surprise. She didn't think I'd remember what my own kids had going on.

She nods. "And the sports sampler."

"The what?" I've never heard of an activity that sounds like an appetizer.

"They play a little of every sport to see what they like. It's easier than having both of them trying full seasons of each sport while I drive all over town."

"You'll still be running around. Let me help. Then they don't have to disrupt the first week by coming to the condo." It's getting harder to call it my place. *This* house has always been my place.

She thinks it over, but her expression doesn't look happy. "I...I could use the time in the evening to keep setting up my business."

I keep my smile just shy of triumphant. I've got another week with them. Another week to woo Natalie. More time to prove myself.

Seven

Simon

Abby and Maddy race up the stairs and run into my condo. "Where's your suitcase, Dad?"

Their shoes pounding on the hardwood floor echo through the empty place. My condo is an old building renovated to capture the old rustic beauty and meld with a new look. High ceilings, exposed brick, and brand-new luxury plank on the floor made it trendy. That wasn't what prompted me to buy it. It was close to my office. Less drive time was less thinking time.

Cool relief wafts over me. I won't have to come here all week.

As soon as Natalie and I told the girls that I'd be staying another week, they wanted to come here and get me packed ASAP. Like me, they're afraid their mom might change her mind. So I gathered them up and gave Natalie some quiet time to get her run in and catch up on some office work.

"Just grab my gym bag." All I need to do is load up on the essentials. I can toss the suits into the garment bag.

When I enter my bedroom, the blinds are half-open, the way the housekeeper always leaves them, as if she knows that it's nice to not walk into a completely dark home. Right now, daylight filters through the tall windowpanes and gets dispersed by the blinds. At night, the streetlights light up the area, but I'm on the third story, so pedestrians can't see inside.

Abby's in the closet, fists on her hips, just like her mom when she's examining a job she doesn't want to do. "We have to take all these?"

Her scowl is on the row of pewter, gunmetal, and navy-blue suits that I wear throughout the week. She's used to seeing me in business wear. Has a week in shorts and T-shirts made that much of an impression?

"Pick five."

A grin breaks out and she sifts through the collection like it's a major decision. I wake up each morning and pick one. Charlie's already paired them with matching shirts and ties.

Ugh. I don't want to put a tie on in the morning. Ties should be outlawed in the summer. But my clients don't want to see my chest poking out in person or in pictures.

My phone goes off. It's rare that Helena calls over messaging or emails.

She starts in as soon as I answer. "There's an expo in town for business executives at the Radisson. Their featured speaker has a family emergency and can't make it. They've contacted the office to see if you can do it."

"Why me?"

She's quiet for a beat and I know I won't like the answer. "Someone recommended you based on the article."

Mr. fucking North Dakota. Naively, I thought the article

was more tongue in cheek, not truly meant to highlight my single status. I don't know about the other bachelors, but it's not exactly something I'm proud of. I liked being married. I liked being married to Natalie. Helena said it's a business expo, so at least the article led to some good promo.

Helena rushes on, knowing full well I don't like how they came to find me—the Mr. North Dakota article. The whole bachelor thing wasn't fully fleshed out when we were approached. "It's the right crowd for you. They're all in various forms of business, but when I inquired, the contact told me that many are entrepreneurs who have started their own. Very few of them have reached the level you have. All you have to do is throw them some inspiration."

Inspiration.

My brother died and left me money. After that, my business really took off, but I haven't brought on more staff and my dad points out how I'm only running a two-person operation.

But if I decline, I'll either look like a diva or an asshole with no time left for the little people. "When is it?"

"The main speaker was scheduled for their evening social on Wednesday evening."

Fuck. The evening? I can't go back on my word after nagging Natalie to let me stay the week. "I have previous obligations. I can do a luncheon."

"Mr. Underwood—"

"It's a luncheon or nothing, Helena. My evenings this week are tied up."

Another two heartbeats of silence. "Is there anything I should know about?"

"It's not work related, no."

"I see," she says stiffly. "I'll call them back and inform them of your availability."

"Thanks." I hang up. Maddy helps me toss in dark socks and underwear for the week. I gather my toiletries so I don't smell like watermelon kids' shampoo every day.

I turn to find the girls making faces in the mirror in the closet. "Ready?"

Maddy twirls like a ballerina. "Where are we going now?"

The drive home will only take fifteen minutes. This errand won't give Natalie nearly enough time to get her stuff done. There's a dessert place downtown we could walk to. "Ice cream?"

"Yeah!" They race for the door.

On our way downtown, I hold their hands. They chatter nonstop, asking me questions about the buildings and what stores and restaurants I've been in.

I realize I'm smiling for no reason other than I enjoy hanging out with my kids. I like doing more than tucking them in at night and rushing back to my computer. I like not shushing them while they're playing in the corner of my office on the weekends.

We're almost to the place I told the girls about when a dark car parks on the street ahead of us. A couple dressed like they're going to the convention Helena called about gets out, peering up at the brick building the girls and I are walking by.

I recognize the man. Mr. Waterson is a client of mine. The woman is much younger than him, but he's never included a Mrs. Waterson in his visits to my office or any correspondence at all.

I should greet them, but my mouth stays closed. What are the chances he'll recognize me? Mr. Waterson isn't my favorite guy to deal with, but he's one of my clients who's been with me the longest, claiming to like my hustle, meaning he likes being able to call me at all hours and get a response.

Like Lancaster, Mr. Waterson has no issues approaching me on weekends. Do I chance that he can casually greet me and let me go about my day?

He looks my way, a disapproving frown tightening his mouth as his gaze sweeps over the girls, especially Maddy, who's hopping beside me. When his gaze lands on me, he's about to look away, but his eyes widen.

"Underwood?"

I use formal titles until I'm told otherwise, like with Lancaster because we're friends, but I've always been Under-wood to Mr. Waterson, who's never asked me to call him William or Bill. "Mr. Waterson. How's it going?" I release my hand from Maddy to give him a perfunctory shake.

His frown deepens and he eyes my hand for a second before he slaps his dry palm into mine for the quickest shake ever. Does he think I'm contagious because I touched a kid? "I certainly didn't recognize you."

I hold my smile in place out of sheer will. He makes it sound like I've committed a felony being out in shorts with my kids on a Sunday. Maddy's hand slips back into mine. "I'm enjoying the day with my girls."

"I see." He gestures to the woman. "Underwood, I don't think you've met Amanda yet. We're looking at buying this building. It's her wedding present."

"Nice to meet you." I don't have to worry about giving up Maddy's hand again. Amanda casts a cool glance our way and goes back to assessing the brick structure.

"Claims she's going to be bored. Wants a special project." Mr. Waterson checks his watch. "The realtor should be here by now. She's going to get a hell of a payoff from this sale, but not if she lollygags."

I evaluate the building. I mean, I bought a house, a nice

home for my family, but not a multistory brick building that houses retail and high-end condos. "This should be a good project."

Maddy tugs on my hand. A family with three kids is leaving the dessert shop, their hands piled full of chocolate, whipped cream and sprinkles. "*Daddy.*"

That earns another dour look from Mr. Waterson. Amanda puts more distance between us. "Just wait, honey." I give Mr. Waterson a smile. "Hope the building works out for you. Let me know if I can be of any help."

"You can help by watching my money. Who's on duty while you're playing dad?" He laughs like it's the funniest joke in the world.

That's not how investment works. Or being a dad. "You're in good hands, Mr. Waterson."

He eyes my clothing. "Amanda showed me that article. I'm wondering if you're as dedicated as you used to be, Mr. North Dakota."

That damn article. "Rest assured, I'm more dedicated to my clients than I ever was."

"Hmmph." His attention is snagged by a car parking across the street. "Finally. I should take an extra percent off her commission."

"Have a nice day." The girls don't need any more prompting to start walking.

Maddy waves to Amanda. "Bye."

Amanda lifts a brow and shifts her gaze to me. Interest infuses her eyes and her icy expression melts into a demure smile.

I give her a nod and look away. The last thing I need is clients thinking North Dakota's most eligible bachelor is hitting on their women—or that I'll hit on my female clients.

Abby leans close and whispers. "I don't like him."

I bend down and whisper back, "When you grow up, you can buy a building for yourself. You don't have to marry a Mr. Waterson."

I'll make sure of it.

* * *

Natalie

I'm sitting in a fabric foldout chair, splitting my attention between Abby running after the soccer ball on the brilliant green soccer field in front of me and catching glimpses of Maddy on the playground.

Rachel sits beside me and after a quick hello and settling in, the story of Simon pours out of me. She's been with me through everything. She was the first one I told about my decision to file for divorce—after my mom found me sobbing on the bathroom floor. It was easier to tell her about that than it is to fill her in on last week and the upcoming week.

"So... he's staying?" Her voice brims with disbelief.

"It's a bad idea, isn't it?"

Her sunglasses aren't dark enough to hide her blink. "Well. It depends."

"Depends on what?" I hang on her answer. We've grown close over the last several months. I was divorcing when her husband was deploying. Our relationship grew deeper and more necessary for each of us. Our circumstances are different, but a lot of our feelings and experiences are the same.

"A few things." She tucks a dark lock of hair behind her ear. Her toddler, Braxton, plays on a blanket in front of us. "First, what each of your expectations are. You expect help.

He says he'll help you, but is he really trying to get back together?"

"I don't know." I haven't thought of Simon's hidden motives. He doesn't usually have any. He sets his goals and he diligently works toward them. For too long, his only goal was to make his business succeed.

Has his goal changed?

No, of course not. But maybe an additional goal? Or maybe he really wants to help me.

"Hold your limits, or it might turn ugly. You had an amicable divorce. I'd hate for it to turn bad because he thought staying the week meant the bedroom door was also open to him."

"He's not like that." The kiss in the office rears up in my memory. I've staunchly repressed it since it happened. "But we did kiss."

She whips her head toward me, her eyes wide. Taking her glasses off, she glances around before she hisses, "What?"

"I mean, he is the most eligible bachelor in the state." My joke doesn't soften her shock.

"Nat. And you let him stay another week?"

I lift a shoulder. "It sort of just happened. We haven't talked about it."

"But he asked to stay after it happened?"

"Yes," I sigh.

"He wants you back."

I know the answer, but that doesn't make it better. "I think so."

"And let me guess—he still has no clue why you presented him with divorce papers in the first place."

"He does." I watch Abby trek across the field. I have a feeling I'll be signing her up for soccer in the fall. "But I don't think he *understands*. It's the weirdest thing. He's so supportive, but he's also clueless when it comes to the circumstances that led to the failure of our marriage."

"Because the marriage served him well. You took care of the kids. You took care of the house and the bills and the running around. He went to work and came home and worked more while you did everything else."

I don't have a reply. Why do I get it, and Rachel gets it, my parents get it, but Simon is alone on an island with nothing but a sense of abandonment? "I can't kick him out now, though. This morning, he worked out at home so I could run to the gym and train with Aleah. Tonight, he's supposed to be around so I can work in the office."

Rachel snorts. "He keeps doing that and *you'll* be the one to suggest another week."

"I can't deny that it's nice to have him around—when he's actually mentally and physically around."

"I miss that."

I send her a sympathetic smile. "Want me and the girls to come by Friday and entertain the kids while you run some errands?" She's starting to shake her head, but I talk over her answer. "Bring the kids to my place. If Friday doesn't work, we're setting a date now."

A smile finally lifts her lips. "Twist my arm. I dream of cleaning the house without them undoing it behind me and just sitting in it for a few hours, enjoying the quiet and the organization."

"Deal. Friday?"

"Friday. But I don't want to interrupt your time."

"Simon won't get home until after six."

Rachel shoots me a side-eye and I realize what I said and how I said it.

"This is hard."

"You still love him." It's not a question.

"It's hard not to. If he had cheated, if he'd been messing

around, if he was an asshole… I could get over him. But he's a good guy."

"You think he's abstained the whole time you've been gone?"

I bristle at her sardonic tone. Simon's a good-looking guy. With a nice body. And a huge bank account. He also has a charming personality to match. "I honestly think so. He's too busy working."

She stares at the girls sprinting across the field. I search the playground and spot Maddy's bright-yellow shirt that I made her wear just so I can pick her out from a distance.

"Would it matter if he did?" she asks. There's genuine curiosity in her voice.

"Yes. Maybe. I don't know."

"Would it matter to him if you had dated between then and now?"

"Maybe. When he commits, he commits hard." It's a trait I used to love about him.

"Okay. So he's staying with you. You've even kissed. He's probably been single the whole time and you have too. What happens if you try to work things out?"

I chew the inside of my cheek as I think, but as always, I come up with the same answer. "He won't divorce Underwood Equity and I can't share my husband."

Rachel pins me with her direct amber stare. "Then set your limits and stick to them, or we're going to recycle the same conversations we had last year, only I think it'll be harder on you to lose him a second time."

Eight

Natalie

Simon's late. He mentioned speaking at a luncheon today but that he'd be around tonight.

I'm making headway on my own business. Last night, I crafted a rough draft of my ad. My heart rate kicks up when I think about posting it.

I have some IRS business to take care of and a new bank account to open. If Simon follows through with all the evenings this week, I can get it done.

Then, I'll be ready to launch in August.

I think about the talk with Rachel a couple of days ago. At soccer, we didn't discuss Simon. There was nothing to discuss. Tuesday was like Monday. He ate the leftovers I had in the fridge for supper and tucked the girls in. The only time I was disturbed was when they came in to give me good-night hugs and kisses.

The clock ticks past seven. I might as well write off tonight.

I herd the kids to their bedroom and we pick up toys.

Abby plops on the floor next to me. "What's wrong, Mom?"

"Nothing. Why?"

She lifts a small shoulder. "Dunno. You just seem sad."

I put my arm around her shoulder. "I'm fine, thanks for asking. Let's get the dirty clothes off the floor and then you two can go take your baths."

Abby jumps up. "I call Mom's bathroom!"

"No fair." Maddy stomps out of the room.

The bathroom fight. I was hoping to skip it just this once. "Whose turn is it?"

"But—" Abby's eyes go wide and she leaps for the door. "Daddy!"

I look over my shoulder. Simon's in the doorway, fielding hugs. His suit jacket is off, the tie is gone, and he's undone the top two buttons of his shirt.

He has a nice chest and I feel every minute that I haven't seen it without a shirt. I rise, so glad to see him that I'm embarrassed. It isn't that I want to rush off to the office. It's that for the third day in a row, he's kept his word.

Is it possible that he can change?

Do I want to risk finding out?

I stuff those questions away. He's done nothing but co-parent all week. We've been little more than two ships coming in and out of the dock at opposite times.

He straightens and leans against the doorjamb. "Sorry I'm late."

His apology is sincere. "There are leftover fajitas in the fridge."

He groans. "That sounds delicious. All right, girls, take your baths, don't argue over the bathroom."

I grin. As if that's really going to work. I leave him to

wrangle bath and bedtime and head to the office. The door clicks shut behind me and it's quiet.

My mind isn't on work. I have a to-do list, but I don't want to look at it. I open my laptop and scroll through the work I've done. The next thing I know, I have the internet pulled up and I'm searching for information about Underwood Equity.

The usual articles about his brother's death appear. The bachelor article. I skip past. I know exactly how eligible he is.

I find an obscure business site with a write-up about the abrupt withdrawal of Brody Waite's interest in the companies Simon was after. My search changes to Brody Waite. There are some old articles about the company he ran with Simon's brother. A feature on his wife and kid.

Is he a workaholic like Simon? Was he and did he change after he married? Does his wife work, or did she give up her life for him?

Nope, she has her own career. She works for an advice column in a national magazine.

I sit back and tap my fingers on the desktop. An advice column. Does she give the advice, or does this Jada person write it? Is Jada real?

My finger has a life of its own as it taps the *Need Advice?* button. A white box pops up.

I chew on my lip. I can't possibly think writing to an advice column will do any good. They probably get so many queries that they can't or don't answer them all.

Still, it can't hurt to write out the conflicting thoughts in my head to a neutral party that doesn't know either of us.

Dear Jada,

I divorced my workaholic husband, but we have two kids. I recently went through a family emergency and he's been a rock. He's even staying with me to help out. And he's actually taking time off work to do it.

We kissed once and I made it clear that it was over between us. But what if it's not? I think we're both starting to wonder if we can make it work if we try again. I can't help but feel like his career would still be his wife and I'll only be the mistress. He's a good guy, or this wouldn't be so hard.

I signed it *Eligible Ex-wife* and left my email for a reply.

My face is hot and I press my hands against my cheeks. I take some deep breaths to slow down the pounding of my heart. I wrote a letter to someone who doesn't know me. My email doesn't have my full last name, but I feel as exposed as if I strolled through the streets naked.

Okay, I have to work.

I pull up my ad and tweak it, then make some copies to adjust them for individual ad platforms. I puff out a breath. The rest of my to-do list doesn't excite me and since I'm emotionally off-kilter, I pick a fun task.

Design a logo.

I haven't stretched my graphic skills in years. An hour has passed when my computer dings. I have an email. Ignoring it, I keep working until I see Jada's Take flash at the top of my screen.

A reply? Already?

Some poor intern is likely assigned to my email, but at least I'm getting a reply instead of seeing it posted on their site.

I pull up their message.

Dear Eligible Ex-wife,

Go with your gut. And by that, I mean your intuition, not the part of you that gets all tingly when he's in the room. Just like women know when their man is cheating and won't change, they know when their guy makes work their identity over being a husband or dad.

Jada's Take

I reread the message. Then, read it again.

Go with my gut.

My common sense tells me he doesn't understand the base of the divorce in the first place. Those parts Jada mentioned absolutely tingle whenever he's around. My hopes are that last week and this week mean something major has shifted inside of him. My heart wants it to be true.

My gut tells me he hasn't changed.

* * *

Simon

"Mr. Waterson wants to be updated on his portfolio." Helena lists another item on her never-ending to-do list. She doesn't even bother to sit down in my office but hovers in the doorway like she's going to make a run for it.

I look at the time. It's almost six thirty. I've managed to get home to give Natalie alone time by seven each night, but one. But every day, it's a juggle. Right as I want to walk out the door, Helena flags me down. I hoped Friday would be different.

"Can you review it and give him a call back?" I scribble a note down to follow up on an earlier meeting with a client.

"He expressly said he wants *you* to review his file and be the one to call him back."

Fucking misogynistic prick. Mr. Waterson and I aren't buds. There's no reason he should insist on only me. I never lose my composure in front of staff so I hold in my insult. "Fine. Pull up his profile."

"Done. There's also a message from Dan Lancaster."

I can guess Lancaster spent the day on the greens with his buddies and is coming at me with horrible investing ideas. Helena's gotten good at assuaging his concerns. "I'll give Mr. Waterson a call. You can take Lancaster and then we can both get out of here."

Her mouth tightens, but she dips her head. She goes back to her desk. I make a mental note to ask her if everything's okay in her talks with Lancaster. He's a micromanager at the core, but I doubt he was rude to her.

I whip through Mr. Waterson's information and give him a call. He boasts about how dedicated we are for working on a Friday night and I let him think that I'm hunkered down at my desk and not one foot out the door.

I hang up with him, shut everything down, and lock up my office. Helena's at her desk with Lancaster on speaker as she reviews his file with him, why we made the decisions we did and why his ideas aren't as profitable.

I give her a wave good night, trusting her to lock up behind me. She dips her head again but focuses on her screen. I'm dismissed.

Fighting residual guilt that her task is taking longer, I drive home. To the house. To Natalie's place. Home sounds better. Couples and families with kids are out everywhere. The days are long this time of year and the evening weather is ideal for just about anything that takes place outside.

When I pull into the driveway, I spot our neighbors from down the road walking my way. Their daughter, who's about Maddy's age, is on a bike, weaving all over the road.

"Simon," Jake calls. "Nice to see you around."

I walk to the edge of the driveway. "I'm helping Natalie out."

"Yeah, she told me about her mother. Glad she's getting better."

"Me too. It takes a lot to get Janie down."

Jake's wife, Sierra, catches her daughter and stops her

before she gets too far ahead. "Your yard was hopping earlier today. She had a friend's kids over and I thought Gemma was going to spring through the yards to come play."

"I doubt Natalie would've minded." It's not my yard anymore, but I hang on the details. My condo's missing this. I don't know my neighbors and I rarely pass them on the stairs, or the few times I take the elevator. I don't know their names and wouldn't recognize them if I passed them on the street.

Here, we know everyone. We even like everyone. Jake threw a neighborhood party two years ago. I missed last summer's, but Natalie said it was a blast.

Jake smiles and puts his hand on his wife's lower back. "We'll let you get going. Just wanted to say hi."

"Nice night for a walk. Enjoy." Glad Jake cut our chat short to spare us all awkwardness about how much I'm helping Natalie, I jog to the door.

The house is quiet, but I listen at the top of the stairs. They're in the movie room.

I leave my suit jacket on a hook by the door and take my tie off. I slip out of my shoes and go downstairs. Natalie's curled up in a plush recliner, with a girl on either side, a bucket of popcorn between them. The kids are in pajamas and their hair's wet and combed out.

"Hi." Natalie pauses the movie. "I don't think I'm up for working tonight. Will you feel terribly taken advantage of if I do movie night instead?"

It sounds like a perfect Friday night. Thank you to Rachel's kids for wearing Natalie out. "Not if I get to join in. Which princess movie is it? Which one has the dog?"

Maddy giggles. "It's *Scooby-Doo*, Daddy."

"I'll go change and be back."

I run up the stairs to my room. Back in my dad uniform

of shorts and a T-shirt, I swing by the kitchen to grab a sandwich and chips for my supper.

By the time I get downstairs, Natalie has sunk lower in her chair and covered herself with a red plaid throw.

When the movie's over, I get the girls to clean up their mess and lead them upstairs. Natalie's dozing, but I'm sure she'll wake up by the time I return. The movie kept the girls up past their bedtime. Combined with the playdate, they're asleep in no time.

I go back downstairs. Natalie's curled into the corner of the recliner, her face peeking out of the top of the blanket. How upset would she be if I took a picture of this? I won't, but it doesn't diminish the yearning to see my wife peacefully sleeping each night.

Do I wake her up? Let her sleep here all night? Carry her to bed?

That would be overstepping my bounds. But she's fallen asleep watching movies before and gets the worst crick in her neck.

Can't have that.

I gently peel the blanket off her. She doesn't twitch. Sliding my arms under her, I lift her to my chest. She resettles in my arms with her head on my shoulder.

Carefully, I make my way to her bedroom without banging her feet on the doorway or walls.

Her side of the bed is rumpled and unmade. I was the bedmaker in the marriage. Easing her into bed, I preserve the memory of how good she feels in my arms.

She moans and rolls on her side. "Don't go."

Did I hear her right? "You want me to stay?"

She pats the other side of the bed. *My* side. "Don't go."

That's all the asking she needs to do. I crawl in beside her but over the covers. I drape the comforter over her and she wiggles until her ass is pressed into my groin.

This might've been a bad idea. The fabric between us is not enough to hide her curves and how perfectly we fit together.

It's going to be a long night.

Nine

Simon

When was the last time I woke up this refreshed?

My awareness rises with each heartbeat. There's a head nuzzling my chest and a leg thrown over my hip. I can barely think with the raging erection sucking up all the blood that should be going to my brain.

I blink my eyes open and inhale the light floral scent of a mass of hair under my chin. My shirt is up and hands are roaming my chest.

I'm in Natalie's bed and she's attacking me.

After her reaction to our kiss, I didn't think she'd be this responsive to waking up and finding out she asked me to stay in bed with her.

She nuzzles my neck and I get painfully harder. A groan rips out of my throat and is met with an approving moan.

She strokes her hands lower and tunnels her fingers between my stomach and waistband. Air freezes in my chest.

Her fingertips brush the tip of my cock. My eyelids drift shut and I thrust my hips into her hand.

Her leg tightens around my waist and the move pulls me into her. I'm putty in her hands, except for one really, really hard body part.

"Yes, Natalie."

She rolls back, her eyes still closed, but she has a sleepy smile. When she cuddles back into my chest, dread creeps in.

She can't... she can't still be asleep... can she?

I shudder when she shoves her hand farther into my shorts. Fuck, it feels so good.

"Natalie?"

All I get is a little murmur.

I catch her arm, but her hand is fisted around my cock. My body's shaking, wanting nothing more than to jack my hips back and forth until I get off in someone else's hand besides my own.

"Natalie," I bark.

She jerks her head back, her eyes bleary but clearing fast.

"Simon!" Her eyes fly wide and she rips her hand away so fast my waistband snaps against the tip of my dick.

"Ow. Shit." I roll to my back. I can't rub my crotch to soothe the burn, so I rock like I'm a turtle stuck on my back. The whole effect diminishes my erection. That's the only saving grace of this moment.

She rolls off the bed and looks down at herself as if she's afraid she's without a stitch of clothing. Her scowl gets directed to me. "What the hell are you doing in my bed?"

"You asked me to stay."

She scoffs and plants her hands on her hips. "When?"

Irritation seeps in. I sit up, wincing at the pinch in my groin. "Last night, when I carried you to bed. You asked me twice."

"I wasn't awake." She says it as if I should've known that

she has complete conversations in her sleep. She never did with me when we were married. Before kids, we woke up frisky and got busy like this morning, but she was always awake.

"How was I supposed to know? You were *talking*."

She shoves her hair off her face, her expression thunderous. "Was I talking this morning?"

I let out a long breath. I can see why she's upset, but I also don't think I did anything wrong. I wanted to. "No. When I saw your eyes were closed..." I shake my head, roll off the other side of the bed and start straightening the sheets and blankets. "I slept on top of the covers, okay? Nothing happened."

Her stance relaxes and she glances toward the open bedroom door. "Good."

A stab of hurt pierces my chest. She can't really be done with me. Just like that? The burn grows and I need space. "I'll go make some breakfast."

"Sure. Yeah." She stabs a hand through her hair to push it off her face. "Um... this weekend isn't your regular weekend with them if you want to head out. I think I've got it from here."

I forget making the bed. She wants me gone?

When I asked to stay here for the week, I assumed the weekend was part of it. I assumed... a lot more than she was ready for, obviously. "I can stay and help all weekend."

She shakes her head but avoids my gaze. "No, but thanks. You'll have the girls next weekend and if you actually do the whole weekend, that'll give me time to catch up."

And if you actually do the whole weekend.

When haven't I? I thought back to my time with the girls. It involved a lot of juggling and sometimes I had to bring them back early to make conference calls. And there were a few trips out of town when I either flew out on Sunday or came back on Saturday.

So, yeah. I stiffed Natalie quite a bit.

"They'll be with me the whole time. Don't worry."

Her expression is dubious, but she nods and escapes to the bathroom. The door clicks shut behind her. A minute goes by and I do nothing but stare at it.

Footsteps and voices echo through the house. The kids are awake. I need to pack. And leave.

My chest tightens until it's hard to draw breath. I need to leave.

But I can hang out while Natalie collects herself. For a couple hours, I can pretend I'm a dad who doesn't have to leave and go days without seeing them when we live in the same town.

My time is cut short. I barely say good morning to the kids when Natalie comes out of the bathroom and announces that she's taking the kids to see Nana.

I give them goodbye hugs and let them help me pack my suits and bags in the car. I send Charlie a message that I'll drop my items off at the dry cleaners so he doesn't look for them when he swaps out clean with dirty suits tomorrow.

The drive to my place sucks. Each mile farther away I get from the house, my mood darkens.

I park in front of the squat, square dry cleaning building and stare out the windshield. People drive by. Adults and kids. Families. Out doing something fun for Saturday.

That could be me.

I yank the car door open and gather my items. A middle-aged woman walking out of the dry cleaners politely holds the door open for me, but her smile fades when she sees the expression on my face. She darts away as soon as I'm clear of the doorway.

My items are left with the teenager stuck with the

weekend shift. I leave and go to my condo. Once I let myself in, I busy myself with unpacking. That takes all of five minutes.

The place is quiet. The traffic noise from outside doesn't make its way in. As old as the building is, the floors don't creak under my feet. There's no laughter. No TV or music from games and toys, and definitely no arguing over who really owns the Harley Quinn doll and, therefore, who gets the rights to play with it whenever they want.

I drop into a chair in the living room. Have I ever sat in this before? Sometimes, I catch the news on the couch. Gazing out the window, I do nothing for a long, long time.

I keep going back to this morning. To the exquisite pleasure of being intimate with my wife. Then to the dawning horror when she realized that I slept with her all night.

Natalie wants me gone. The thought of being intimate with me affects her so much she'd rather not have me around.

Being intimate with me affects her.

Three times now, she's responded to me. Both in mind and body, though her conscious mind overrides it all.

She's still attracted to me.

A small smile creeps along my lips. I can work with that.

Natalie

The weekend without Simon sucks. There's no sugarcoating it. No pretending that I'm fine, that the girls and I do just fine, and life from here on out is awesome.

It's like those first months alone after Simon moved out. I'm hovering just above being despondent and the girls are clingier. Needier. Every time I sit down, one of them is on me. If I get up to try to do laundry, I can't turn a corner without tripping on them. I finally give up trying to do anything productive and we head down to our home theater.

This time, they pick a *Lego* movie and I don't have to ask why. Simon loves the *Lego* movies. I don't pay attention to the show but hug the girls as they cuddle with me and space out on the screen.

I woke up with my hand down his shorts.

He claimed I asked him to stay with me all night. I believe him. He's never lied about that stuff before. And how many times have I gone to bed wishing he was there?

Was I really attacking him while I was asleep?

Was I really asleep?

Thinking back to this morning, my cheeks warm. I was in that stage of sleep and awake and very aware that someone I'm limitlessly attracted to was in bed with me.

His body was so hard. And his—yeah. That was hard too.

The phone saves me from continuing down that path. Until I look at the caller ID. Simon.

I ease out from under the girls and crouch on the stairs. A wall blocks the worst of the sound and the girls won't hear what I'm saying.

"Hey," Simon says after I answer. "I wanted to touch base about this week."

Part of me is disappointed. His tone is gentle, not his usual brusque and businesslike one, but he's still talking logistics. This isn't an *I want you back* call. As if that would be better.

"Yes. I'll drop them off Wednesday when you're done with work."

"I can pick them up."

So seeing his car in the driveway and him walking through the house can mess me up? Wednesday's too soon to withstand that. "We'll be out and about. I can drop them off."

"Okay. About the weekend…"

I squeeze my eyes shut. He's going to ditch them. I'll have to deal with the questions and the feelings of insecurity when I tell the girls—both mine and theirs. I was right to ask him to leave.

"Lancaster is giving Helena a hard time and I think it's best to meet him in person. Play a few rounds of golf and get a feel for what his friends are telling him that contradicts so badly with me."

"Doesn't Lancaster live in town?"

"He's in Arizona year-round now." My hopes are dropping that this isn't the brush-off I think it is. I'm already mentally working through my free time the next week and when I can get into the office for my own work when Simon clears his throat. "Do you guys want to come with me?"

I blink at the wall. Tiny giggles filter out from the movie room. "All of us?"

"Yeah. It'll just be me. Helena's going to stay back and deal with anything else that comes up. But we can get a suite with separate rooms and you guys can do what you want while I talk to Lancaster."

I want to say yes so badly, but I make myself slow down and think it through. Helena won't be with us. That would help make it feel like less of a family vacation and more of a work trip where he brings the kids. Regardless, I won't be totally tied to Simon and his schedule. Me and the girls would be free to do what we want.

I feel like it's crossing a line, but I can't figure out where the line is. When Simon travels on the weekend, it's all about work—even when we were married. There was no traveling with babies or packing us all up and going. This is a first.

"We'd be coming home on Sunday?" It's like I'm trying to find a reason to say no, like missing a day of sports sampler camp would be a deal breaker to give the girls a unique travel experience.

"Yes. I can't rush this thing with Lancaster. I might be out on the greens each morning, but he works remotely throughout the week."

But the afternoon would be too hot to golf. At least, I assume so. I haven't been to Arizona and I don't golf. Simon mastered golf in college after he heard that tennis and golf are stellar networking events and where a lot of major business decisions are made. He's passable in tennis too.

"Okay. Yeah. It'll be fun to get a mini vacation."

He goes quiet. "We weren't very good at taking vacations before, were we?"

"Work always comes first." And there was no one to take over. There still isn't.

Once I was busy with kids, most of the load fell on Simon. If Helena had been around then, we could've snuck away, but hiring a full-time employee, one with the salary needed to recruit someone knowledgeable and experienced, wasn't an option until after Hayes died.

Simon ignores the dig about work. "We'll fly out Friday. Charlie's arranging the flight and hotel. I'll have him send you the details."

A tendril of hurt snakes through me. His assistant has to deal with me. It's exactly the distance I asked for and don't want.

"Okay."

"And Natalie." There was a note of caution in Simon's tone. "I may be at Lancaster's beck and call. Don't make plans around me. I want you guys to have fun."

"We'll make it work."

We disconnect. He expected me to say no, but I can't. He's making an effort. For someone married to his work, asking to bring the kids on a work trip, especially with an account that's as critical as Lancaster's, is a huge step.

Without seeing old friends, Arizona is definitely better than moping around the house, doing laundry and arranging gear for the sport of the week. Speaking of which, it's T-ball week. I need to find baseball gloves. I have a small pink one that Abby used when she was in T-ball. I need to find the one that'll fit Maddy.

Then I'll have to think about packing. With my parents living in the same city, there's little reason to travel. But this weekend, we're flying out. Giddiness prompts a smile. I haven't gone out of town in so long. Simon's parents are rarely in the country and when they are, they land in Fargo for a kiss-kiss hug-hug *we're so busy we must leave immediately* visit. They love their grandchildren, but not enough to spend time with them when it means tolerating me. I refuse to send my kids to grandparents who don't respect me.

I walk back into the room where the *Lego* movie is still going strong with a smile on my face. Do I tell the girls?

Or do I wait? Simon's notorious for plan changes. But after the last two weeks, I feel like he'll move heaven and earth to make this weekend happen. And what's worse, if he does, it'll only be harder for me and my heart. Because then I'll start to think that he's really changed and my heart will ignore my gut.

Ten

Simon

Sweat trickles down my back. Dry heat or not, it's fucking hot.

The greens are packed with everyone else who thinks it's a good idea to golf in the early morning hours at the most shaded golf course in Phoenix.

I wipe my brow and chug another bottle of water. Since I've had a few and don't have to piss, I drink another.

Lancaster squints, crow's-feet winging out from under the brim of his ball cap. "Hope you skipped the coffee this morning."

"I can't imagine drinking anything hot before coming out here."

He chuckles and selects an iron from his bag. I'm shamelessly taking refuge under the canopy of the golf cart. The two other guys we're golfing with are somewhere on the hole. Lancaster hung back to wait for me.

For older men carrying a decent beer gut on each of

them, they can out-golf the hell out of me. Lancaster adjusts the elastic waistband on his white shorts. He must have a tan line from his shins to his midthighs, thanks to his shorts and high socks. He's always reminded me of Natalie's dad.

Only Natalie's dad isn't so paranoid about my business acumen.

I spend holes one through fourteen talking about how I select investments, who I invest with, how I'm expanding my firm, and why their ideas don't work as well for my business model. There's no animosity or confrontation. I get the impression that this is a group that misses the fast-paced, high-stakes work life and lives vicariously through whoever will talk to them.

One of Lancaster's buddies is talking real estate with one of the ladies from a group that's in front of us at the holes. Their group is an identical version of the one I'm with. Retirees who hang out and live vicariously through each other's work war stories.

Not that I mind golf, but I'm over it for the whole weekend and for the rest of the summer. It's hot, while the hotel I left has air conditioning and a whirlpool that I fantasize is filled with cool water for soaking my hot and sweaty balls.

I also imagine asking Natalie to join me, but that's a different problem and one I can't think about while surrounded by retired individuals.

"You should apply another round of sunscreen." Lancaster's standing in the shade of the golf cart.

"Good idea." I stand clear of the cart and reapply sunscreen to all exposed skin. "What's there to do in Phoenix on Saturday afternoons that's good for kids?"

Lancaster's brow furrows. "You brought your kids?" He doesn't sound disapproving, and that's why I like Lancaster, even though he's a pain in the ass. His kids are grown, but he's always talking about his grandkids and asking about Abby and Maddy. "Is Natalie here too?"

"Yes, they're all here." I slide the sunscreen canister back into my borrowed golf bag's pouch. "I don't know if I ever mentioned it, but Natalie and I got divorced."

"Aw hell. I'm sorry to hear that. When she left the company, I just thought with the kids..." He waves to a group in front of us, his expression solemn. "But you brought her here? When did you get divorced?"

This might be crossing boundaries with a client, but I married young and worked all the time. My friends list is short. "Last fall."

"Divorced that recently and she still flew with you here?" When I nod, his eyes shine with approval. "Good, I guess. My first wife made me pay for working too much. I almost made the same mistake with Peggy, but by then, I'd made enough money to slack off and hire more people. It's tough when you're just starting out."

I feel more like a weathered veteran, but Lancaster has owned various companies for the last forty years. He's continued to dabble in real estate and investments with Peggy. They're actually Peggy's holdings, but once Lancaster retired, she allowed him to partner with her.

"It's not easy." Now we're stuck waiting for the other group to make it through the sixteenth hole, but I sense Lancaster wants the privacy.

"Why don't you guys come out to my place?"

What would Natalie think? She enjoyed Lancaster and could talk him down much better than Helena, but I don't want to decide for her. "I'd have to ask her."

"You do that. Tell her that we have a pool the girls can play in and it's even shaded. I'll grill. It'll be a blast. Peggy's having grandkid withdrawals." He snorts. "No one wants to visit us in the summer. Can you believe it?"

Since I'm about to disintegrate into a pile of ash, yes, my northern climate ass can believe it. "Since we have time, I'll give her a call."

To get a little privacy, I have to step out of the shade. I'm wearing a Lancaster Industries hat that was waiting for me when I arrived, but the sun beats down on me.

When Natalie answers, loud voices echo on the other end. "What's up?"

"Lancaster invited us over for the afternoon. Do you have plans already?"

"Is it a business thing?" The phone gets muffled as she calls after one of the girls. "Quit putting your face against the glass. They don't like that."

My guess is they're looking at snakes or frogs. There's no animal that can repel the girls. My gut twists as I look around. I'd rather be at the zoo with them. I'm missing their awe over animals they've never seen before. "No. He said Peggy is going through grandkid withdrawal and would love to have us over."

"I miss talking to Peggy," she says wistfully. "Do they know we're..."

Divorced. "Yes. He's impressed that you can stand me."

That gets a chuckle from her. "I always did like him. Oh, thank you for breakfast this morning."

"Anytime." Before I left, I arranged for room service with all their favorites for when I knew they'd be awake.

"They have a pool." Everyone has a pool here, but I really want this visit with Natalie. It's a trip I can give her and the girls. I won't exactly be working.

"The hotel has a pool, but I've been informed that it looks boring. Sure. Let's do it. I was going to head back to the hotel soon anyway. We're all wilting."

After I hang up, I let Lancaster know we're on.

He grins. "I knew I liked you. I'm glad you came. Helena's... she's not the same as you and Natalie."

Helena's professional to the bone and probably doesn't swap the best steak seasoning stories with the avid griller. "She's focused."

"Yeah. You both need to learn there's more to life than work." He shoots me a knowing look. "Learn before it's too late."

"I think that ship has sailed."

He adjusts his white hat, which doesn't have sweat stains on it. Either he's impervious to the heat, or he swaps it out every week. My hat will have to be burned after today. "Whether you and Natalie work things out, and let's face it, the divorce is kind of a final sign, take heed. It feels like work gives you everything. Money that brings opportunity that brings a life you never expected. But it doesn't tuck you in at night. It's not there when you're sick. It doesn't care if it's your birthday or whether you celebrate Christmas or Hanukkah. Work can wait."

The guy that's been sucking up all our weekend concentration just told me work can wait? I need to let it go, but I don't. "What about those weekend emails I keep getting?" My tone is light, but I have to fight to keep the irritation from showing in my face.

Lancaster's face screws up like he doesn't know what I'm talking about. "I email when I think about it. You don't have to answer right away. They have autoresponders nowadays. Peggy has one for weekends, holidays, evenings, you name it. Her auto-response is that we'll be back during such-and-such hours. You should try it sometime. Oop, they're done."

I'm left scowling at him as he trots to set his golf ball in place and gazes to where he wants it to go.

You should try it sometime. Lancaster has all his money

in the bank or is continually growing it with me. His kids are adults and he has enough to set his five grandkids up for life.

I'd love to try it sometime. If only it was that simple.

* * *

Natalie

Peggy greets me with a giant hug. I can only return the embrace with one hand. Maddy clutches my other hand. Abby's holding Simon's.

"It's so good to see you again." Sincerity pours out of her. Unlike a lot of Simon's clients, what you see with Peggy is what you get. She cuts to the point but is tactful, is unashamed about her love of money and numbers and how to grow them bigger, and she enjoys life.

"I'm happy this worked out."

Peggy steps back to ooh and ahh over Abby and Maddy. "Look at you two. Little holograms of your parents. Look one way and you resemble your dad, look another way and it's your mom."

Maddy's nose scrunches at the hologram part, but she likes being on the receiving end of gushing.

Simon introduces them. "I know you haven't seen them since they were babies."

"And what cute babies you both were." She waves us in. "Leave your shoes on. We'll go right out to the pool. Dan has everything set up to grill and we have the misters going to beat the heat away."

I always forget that Lancaster's first name is Dan. He said he went by Dan all his life until he met Peggy. Her first husband was also named Dan, so her family called Lancaster by his last name. It stuck.

We follow Peggy through the house. Unlike the cream stucco exterior, the inside is a colorful mix of family photos, trinkets that were clearly made by someone under ten, and travel souvenirs. The Lancasters are doing retirement right. This is the first major trip that Simon and I have taken. Ever. For our honeymoon, we were moving from Wharton University to Fargo. After that, we had a fledgling business.

We'd talked about it. Constantly. During the summer, when we couldn't afford to go anywhere farther than our backyard, we'd sit on the porch and sip a beer, daydreaming about all the places we'd go. Then we bought the house, knowing full well that it was our vacation home and holiday home wrapped in one family home. We chose roots over wandering, but we never quit thinking that one day, we'd reach a point where we covered mortgage payments *and* had enough to take the kids around the world.

That wasn't going to happen on one income. Simon's income. My house was paid off, thanks to the divorce. I know Simon has plans for their college fund, and my pride says that if we're flying somewhere for nothing but fun, I'm going to earn it. We won't be cruising on Simon's dime.

He's not the only one who wants to prove himself in the world.

We step out the sliding doors to the back patio. I expect a wave of heat, but the shade cover is deep and clouds of cool mist hover between me and the water. The pool's inviting glitter takes my mind off the temperature.

"Nat," Lancaster greets me warmly and folds me into a hug.

"Thanks for the invite."

"When I heard you were in town, I knew both Peggy

and I wouldn't want to miss you. It was generous of your husband to fly out and humor this old guy."

I grin, suspecting half the reason Lancaster was so insistent was that he missed the hour-long appointments and long lunches with Simon. I used to be a part of those once upon a time.

Peggy points out the bathroom and the pool toys and it's no time before the girls jump into the pool and happily splash around. I don't have to be on as high alert. The pool has a wide set of stairs and a solid railing to enter and exit the shallower end.

Simon and Lancaster retreat to the grill that's a little farther from the house but still shaded. Peggy sets out lemonade with ice and a tray of sugar cookies.

I'm about to take a seat when Peggy whips her top off to reveal a sleek black bathing suit. "I hope you plan to swim as well. It didn't get as hot out as the weatherman predicted."

I'd hate to know what that was. A swim sounds nice after a day of roaming the zoo. "I just might." I packed my suit but didn't plan to swim. I bring it as more of a precaution since Maddy's often too short to touch the bottom, depending on the pool.

"There's a changing room inside. Just take a right. It's the first door past the dining room."

I disappear inside and change and fight a case of nerves. Wrapping a towel around my waist, I head back out. Peggy's towing Maddy on a floating lily pad and Abby's showing Simon how she can flip in the water.

He's grinning when he glances my way. He does a double take and his smile fades as heat infuses his dark eyes. I'm wearing a tankini. It's nothing terribly revealing. My arms are nothing like Aleah's carved muscle and I still have the same post-childbirth pooch that I had the last time Simon and I were intimate.

I can't say since the last time he saw me naked because that was only a few weeks ago.

I drop the multicolored polka-dot towel across a lounge chair and step into the water. It's cool and refreshing. Thankfully, I put my hair in a tight bun this morning, and I dip in until my chin hits the surface.

Out of the corner of my eye, I can tell Simon's still watching me. Lancaster is talking to him while waving his grill tongs, oblivious to the lack of attention.

I cock a brow at Simon and flick my gaze to Lancaster as if to say *pay attention to our host*. But Simon's eyes narrow slightly. He doubles down on his focus and my stomach flutters.

I'm not going to win in an intense stare-off with him. I turn my back and glide toward Peggy and Maddy. Abby's swimming around them now.

Peggy releases Maddy's lily pad to Abby and the girls play together. I stay crouched in the water next to Peggy.

"I'm sorry to hear about the divorce," she says, so only I can hear. "It's nice to see you two can be more than civil."

"Yeah." It's hard not to be way more than civil. Who knew that'd be my problem? A sigh escapes. "I wish..."

"Don't I know it." Peggy surreptitiously glances at Lancaster and lowers her voice even more. "I served Dan with papers. A year after we were married."

My brows pop up. I'm friendly with the couple, but not to this level. "What happened? Or didn't happen?"

"His life was work. I don't even know how he found time to date me and get married. But it wasn't two months in that I realized everything his first wife said was true." She chuckled. "Well, not all of it, but she was justifiably angry. It was a wake-up call for me. My first marriage dissolved because my ex felt neglected. I thought he was whining. I ate a lot of humble pie and tried to force-feed it to Dan."

"It must've worked."

"No. He thought I had the problem. So I moved out."

I could picture Peggy packing her bags, taking half the pantry and every piece of furniture she considered hers. "And that got to him?"

"No."

I'm riveted to the story. It's similar to my own. Only Peggy and Lancaster obviously succeeded where we failed. "Then how..."

She smiled, the memory clearly a fond one. "We met with the divorce lawyer, signed the papers, then as we're leaving and my heart's been trashed, his lawyer grins and looks him in the eye. I'm not even out of the room and he says, 'Call me when you get sick of wife number three.'"

I sputter, shocked at the comment. "Rude."

"Oh, it pissed Dan off. But it also dawned on him that if he didn't change, he was going to be alone with only a trail of broken hearts to show for it. He demanded the papers back, ripped them up and said to me, 'Whatever it takes.' So we outlined rules—for both of us." She lifts a shoulder. "And here we are."

I eye Simon. His hand is shoved in his pocket and he's loosely holding a longneck beer in his other hand. He doesn't notice me watching him, and I look away before he can catch me and get the wrong impression.

Setting limits with Dan worked because it dawned on him exactly what was wrong and that he played an important role, both in causing it and fixing it. Simon hasn't reached that stage and I don't know that he can.

I give Peggy a sad smile. "I should've used your lawyer."

Eleven

Simon

"Dad, I'm bored." Maddy's on her stomach on my office floor. It's Friday night and close to their bedtime. I had a long call and alternated between muting it and either bribing the girls with treats to stay quiet while I talked or threatening to tell their mother they didn't behave and they'd lose out on activities.

The last one was totally a bluff. Natalie would think it was my fault I had them at the office late. But I can't expect clients who invest millions with me to work around my time zone. Their money means I'm at their beck and call.

I type up notes and reminders for me and Helena to split a little work tomorrow so neither one of us is tied up all day on a Saturday. "Okay, we're ready to go."

Maddy pops up, but Abby's slow to roll off the floor. Her shoulders are slumped and her mouth is turned down like she tasted something awful.

She presses a hand to her gut. "I don't feel so good."

I'm about to tell her that we'll go straight to my place when she doubles over and vomits. I leap for the trash can as Maddy backpedals toward the door.

"Shit." I didn't mean to swear. "Dammit." Still swearing. I shut up and thrust the can toward Abby. She hugs it and continues throwing up.

The smell of rancid puke fills the air.

Maddy jumps up and down, shaking her hands. "Ew."

"Wait out by Helena's desk, Mads." I roll the chair my clients use toward Abby. "Sit."

She nods, her chest heaving. I press a hand to her head. She's not hot, but she's clammy. "I'll clean up the worst." Then I'll call Charlie to get our cleaning service in here to work their magic—and pay them extra.

I've never been more grateful that I kept the original hardwood when I bought the space than as I use all the paper towels from the restroom. I save some to wipe off my shoes and go into the hallway. The bank in the same building has long since closed, but there's a public bathroom between my section and theirs. I steal all their paper towels and wet some down.

As I'm cleaning the floor, Abby groans. "I want to go home."

"After I get this and bag up the trash, we'll go back to my place. We can stop for some ginger ale and crackers."

She lets out another long moan. "No. I want to go *home*."

I don't push it. She feels like shit and my place isn't her home. I call Charlie with the SOS and then call Natalie.

"Abby threw up and she wants to go home."

"Yeah, okay. Is she alright? How's Maddy?"

"So far, so good, but this came on really sudden." I make a note to grab an empty trash bag—make that two—for the ride to Natalie's. "I'm almost done cleaning up here and then we'll head out."

"Did she throw up on the furniture?"

"No, we're at the office."

"This late on a Friday?"

I don't respond. What can I say? It's nine on a Friday night. This is how I party. This is how I've spent Fridays since I met Natalie.

"Never mind. Just get her home. I'll run a bath for her."

I load the girls. Maddy sits as close to her door as she possibly can, but she clutches a clean trash bag in her hand. Abby's staring woodenly out the window, her face pale.

As soon as I park in the driveway, Abby heaves into her bag. I rush out of the car and open the back door. I catch Maddy's wide eyes. "Go inside and let Mom know we're here."

She nods and scurries off, forgetting to shut her door. I unbuckle Abby. She's retching and trying to catch her breath.

"It's okay, honey. I'll carry you in." I lift her out and adjust her slight weight. Natalie's behind me when I turn.

"There's a bath waiting for her and a laundry basket outside the door for her clothes." She wrinkles her nose. "And your clothes."

I smell like puke. My car smells like puke. My office will smell like puke until the morning. "Do you mind grabbing my gym bag? I'll shower and change."

She does as I ask and closes and locks the car. Inside, we work as a team. She undresses Abby and I strip down and take our dirty laundry downstairs, including Maddy's, who's already in pajamas and snuggled into bed.

I tuck my suit in a bag to go to the cleaners and start the washer. By the time I'm upstairs, Natalie's getting Abby out of the tub.

"Can I use your shower?" I call from outside the cracked open door.

"Go ahead."

I want to tuck both girls in, even if Maddy's already asleep, but I don't want to leave the lingering smell of vomit in their room.

Running through the shower, I use the products that remind me of my wife and how much I love her smell. The towel I use is achingly familiar. I bought some cheap towels when I first moved, lacking any sense whatsoever of what makes a good towel.

I'm back in my shower, in my house, with sick kids. The sense of normalcy sneaks in like a siren's call I'd gladly steer my ship toward. Only it's temporary.

Dressed in my gym shorts and a T-shirt, I go out to the living room. Natalie's perched on the edge of the couch, scrolling through her phone. Her hair is unbound and in a messy halo. She's got color in her face from spending time outdoors.

The picture of her in her swimsuit has been stuck in my head all week. I'm confident I've never seen that suit. Nothing could distract me from the sight of her in it. Pale-pink top and yellow-and-pink-striped bottoms. Every freckle scattered over her shoulders has been long seared into my memory.

Will this wanting ever end? If she's done with me, it's the cruelest punishment but one I'm willing to bear. I haven't given up on her, on us, but she needs more time than I thought. It's only been weeks, but it's enough to make me wonder if I'm on a fool's mission. The only one not to know it's doomed for failure.

"Are they awake?" I ask.

She shakes her head. "Maddy's out and Abby was asleep by the time I got back with the puke bucket." The old silver basin that we scavenged while cleaning out her grandma's place after the funeral is the designated puke bucket.

"I'm glad we came here. I don't think I'm prepared with even one bucket."

She smiles. "Good thing you had a gym bag."

I shove my hand through my wet hair. The living room clock says it's almost ten. "I should get going. Let you get some rest."

She waves toward the guest room across from the girls' room. "Go ahead and stay. They'd be gutted to miss their weekend with you."

"You mind? I'd hate to miss my weekend with them too." I mean it. I had a weekend full of activities that they've already done over the years but that they never seem to tire of. The splash pad and the place that's like a science center and a playroom had a baby, and of course the zoo because there's at least one stuffed animal I haven't bought for them.

Speaking of which. "If they're feeling better tomorrow, I can take them back to my place. Or I'll go grab their things."

"Maddy didn't mention Pink Kitty, so she must've been tired."

I stand for a moment. Natalie looks around the living room. I felt like I was back at home in the bathroom, but now I'm a fish floundering onshore. "Night, Natalie."

The corner of her mouth hitches up. "Good night, Simon."

I trudge up to the guest bedroom. The mission of winning my wife back is sinking terribly. I need to step up my game. If it was a start-up seeking investors, I'd pass on it without a second thought. Not a chance that'll earn any money for me or them.

But Natalie's nothing like work. She's more precious than any company I invest in, and I have no idea how I can win her back.

* * *

Natalie

A retching noise wakes me. I sit straight up, like a mummy coming to life, and blink.

A light flips on across the house, the glow invading my room.

Now I hear coughing.

"Shit." I vault out of bed and rush to the girls' bedroom, glad I wore longer pajama shorts than the boy shorts I usually wear. My shirt is baggy, but I put on an old and worn sports bra that I can sleep comfortably in.

Abby's curled in the corner of her bottom bunk, moaning. Simon's halfway up the ladder, holding the silver basin for Maddy.

He looks at me, his face ashen. The smell is atrocious, but nothing we haven't tackled before. We fall back into our *the kids are sick* roles. He lifts Maddy down and carries her to the bathroom. I strip her and wash her down while he gathers all of her bedding.

He appears at the bathroom door with fresh pajamas and helps me dress her. The pile of dirty laundry grows. When Maddy's in fresh clothes, Simon picks her up. She snuggles against his shoulder. The way he cradles her like he did with Abby yesterday makes me pause. Seeing how excellent he is with them has always been a weak spot for me.

I grab new sheets and make Maddy's bed, finding an extra blanket. He tucks her in while I find another bucket.

"I hope that's the end," he whispers as he steps off the bunk ladder.

Then Abby moans and rolls over, searching for the silver

basin. I dive for her and make it just in time. While I sit with her, Simon goes to the bathroom to get a washcloth.

Once we get Abby cleaned and settled and wash her bucket, Simon gathers up the laundry. It's spilling over his arms and he's going to need a shower. I'll have to clean myself and wash up too.

"I got this," he says. "Go get some rest. We don't know when it'll hit again."

I puff hair out of my eyes. "Do you need something else to wear?" Unless he left clothes here, I don't have much to offer. My baggiest clothes would be skintight on his tall, wide-shouldered frame.

"I'll dry the underclothes I wore under my suit while I shower. Don't worry." His smile is reassuring. "Rest. We might need it."

I wash up and change pajamas. Simon's quiet, but my senses are attuned to him moving through the house. I hear the other shower kick on and off. He goes back downstairs, comes up, and then the door to his room closes.

I'm not tired. I don't know how long I stare at the ceiling, recalling how good of a partner he is at times like this. Finally, my eyes drift shut. I don't know how much sleep I get before there's a repeat.

This time, it's just Maddy and she's good about getting to the bucket. There's nothing sexy about this detail, but Simon's tight undershirt and boxer briefs are hard not to notice. His powerful thighs are usually hidden by his basketball shorts—poorly, but it's something. His gym shirts are baggy, but this undershirt practically takes a highlighter to his defined pecs and the hard planes of his stomach.

When everything's cleaned up and Maddy's settled, we step out of the room. He rolls his shirt up and rips it over his head. He's in nothing but his underwear and his hair is rumpled. This is the Simon I wanted more of when we were married. Casual. More than casual.

I can't keep my gaze from dipping to his chest. *Damn.* He's in maroon boxer briefs with a black waistband. I'm wearing powder-blue pajama pants with pandas on them and a top that falls off one shoulder. He's granite and I'm a dandelion field gone to seed.

I bite the inside of my lip to keep from swearing. I used to climb every inch of him. Tasting, licking, nibbling. He was mine. Cleaning up sick should've kept my mind off of this.

"I don't think I got hit, but I want to keep my bedding clean. It's probably time to put another load in."

I step back so he can go around me. "Thanks for doing the laundry."

"No problem." He grins, looking like he got eight hours of sleep and not three hours of broken rest. "Don't take this the wrong way, but I hope I don't see you before morning."

My smile comes easy. He heads to the basement and I go back to my bedroom. I stand inside the doorway. If there's another incident, he's going to need a change of clothes. Maybe I have something he can wear.

I scour my closet, starting in the deepest corners and lesser-used drawers. The sad fact is that his half of the closet is still empty, as are the drawers he used in the dresser. But just in case something of his got stuck with mine, I look anyway.

I hit pay dirt at the bottom of the closet. A pair of black cloth shorts is hidden in the shadows, along with an old shirt. They're partially concealed by the ironing board I do my best to never have to use.

The light by the guest room is still on. I hear soft footsteps coming up the stairs. I can catch him before he goes into his room.

I'm looking at my find clutched in my hand when I walk out. I glance up, searching for him. "Hey, look what I found—"

I gasp. He's half turned, frozen at the base of the stairs that go up to the bedrooms. His ass is on full display and he's not wearing one stitch of clothing. "Natalie, shit, sorry." He cups his balls and as he does his ass tightens.

A small moan leaves me. He looks so damn good naked. Two weeks ago, I had my hand on that impressive length he's cupping. Seeing him like this makes the feel of him blaze to life across my fingertips. Hard erection, covered by soft, blistering-hot skin.

"Here." I thrust the clothes out and try to avert my eyes, but they go to the sliding doors instead, the kind with the blinds between the panes. With the blinds closed, the reflected image of him is erotically clear. The angle is different and he's posed like a marble statue, cupping his privates. I squeeze my eyes shut. My nipples are painfully hard and I hope my sorry excuse of a sports bra is enough to hide them. "I found these at the bottom of the closet."

He lifts them from my grip. "I, uh, forgot the other pair of underwear in the room and thought you all were asleep so I could sneak back." His voice is rough. Is it awkward for him, or is he burning up like me?

"You shouldn't sneak around naked. The girls could be up any time."

"You're right. Bachelor habits, I guess." Those words stab me in the chest. He rushes on. "I promise I don't do this when they're at my place."

"I know." Abby and Maddy are deep asleep and their door is mostly closed. I doubt they would've awoken during the ten seconds it would've taken him to get to his room from downstairs. But the longer I keep him, the more we risk them waking. "I'll let you, um, get dressed."

His grin is devilish. "What if I have nothing to wear?"

My pulse quickened. "My shorts would be really short on you, but you do have nice legs."

"If that's the case, I can take the ones you're wearing."

I flutter my fingers against my chest over my racing heart. I always enjoyed banter with Simon, but we might have a long night ahead of us. "I think you'll figure something out."

"Sure. And don't worry about the morning. I'll get up with them. Get some rest. Sleep tight, Natalie."

The slight tease to his words is enough incentive for me to keep my eyes off him. I spin around and charge back to my room.

Sleep tight, Natalie.

Letting me sleep in after a puke fest. I'd rather have that than a dozen roses any day.

Twelve

Natalie

Saturday was *a day*. Simon and I did nothing but cater to sick kids and keep up with laundry. There was a mighty heave session before bed and we have more laundry to do on top of the normal weekend stuff. But since then, we haven't been plagued with new stomach incidents.

The girls woke up feeling normal but worn out. They're planted in front of the TV in the living room, nestled in blankets with books, markers and notepads piled around them. Yesterday, Simon ran and grabbed the girls' bags and stuffed animals. Today, he's out getting some groceries, mostly crackers and Sprite.

Simon and I aren't feeling queasy or affected. They must've picked up the stomach bug from the play area I took them to on Friday before I dropped them off with their dad.

Guilt only affects me because the kids are miserable, but I can't deny that being surrounded by my family all weekend was nice. I didn't get much work done, but I wouldn't have if I was alone and dealing with all of this.

Simon was with me every step of the way. And I recalled how he was always there with me when things got tough. It never mattered that he worked all day or had meetings. He never held that over my head when the kids were up sick all night or when they woke with growing pains or nightmares. He was out of bed and taking care of them with me.

It was the normal day-to-day issues that he failed at.

I scrub my face and get up. The longer I sit here and ponder how different things have been since my mom was sick, the more confused I'm going to get. Simon's made no more moves to get close to me and we'd even taken the Arizona trip together and stayed in the same suite—with him in a separate bedroom.

Yeah, not a fun train of thought. There's always laundry.

I go to my bedroom, gather my dirty clothes and bedding from the previous week and carry them to the basement. My mind loses its attempts to quit thinking about Simon, inconveniently getting stuck on his bare ass in the night-light.

Is he done with me? There was the kiss in my office and then the night he slept in the same bed, but since I shut him down, he's respected my limits. Dammit.

What do I think? That I'm so irresistible he can't keep his hands off me no matter what I say? I'd be angry at him all over again if he did. But he's not pursuing me, and the echoes of hurt from being so easily resisted make no sense.

That ass, though. And his chest.

I push my hair off my face and punch the buttons on the machine. When it starts to make noise, I turn around and slump against it. I'm not ready to go upstairs and pretend to be the mom who has her shit together. I'm a woman mixed up over a guy and I thought I wouldn't be that person after I said *I do*. I wasn't even that person when I said *I don't*. Then, I was only a mom trying to do her best for her kids. A mom who was trying to find her inner woman again and unearth the goals I want in my life.

Things are exactly as I need them. Simon's co-parenting. I managed to get to two personal training appointments last week and have been doing my training runs in the morning. And I've almost nailed down the design for my logo.

But there's a huge gaping hole in my life in the exact shape of a sexy man with a devilish smile who can wear the hell out of a suit.

The laundry door pushes open and Simon enters with a small armful of girl clothes. My heart stutters. He hasn't shaved all weekend and the faint dusty brown stubble on his chin gives him an irresistible, rugged look.

He takes one look at my face and hip checks the door closed. "What's wrong?"

I shake my head and fold my arms like they're some sort of defense against how devastating he looks in his gray gym shorts and red T-shirt. The clothes I found in the closet are currently in the dryer. "Nothing. I just needed a moment."

He dumps the clothes in the dirty pile against the wall. The laundry is noisy, but it's cocooning us in our own space and the extra heat thrown off from the dryer increases my antsy discomfort. It has nothing to do with the man in front of me causing a full-body flush.

Towering over me, he rests one hand on the washer lid next to me. The faint vibrations of the machine are nothing I've noticed before, but his proximity amplifies the effect until I'm ready to strip down to nothing in a desperate attempt to seek relief.

"I should go then," he says quietly. "To give you a moment."

He doesn't move and I don't ask him to. "Stay."

The corner of his mouth slowly lifts. "Are you sure? Remember what happened the last time you asked me to do that?"

I wrapped my hand around his cock and that was only the beginning of what my dreams had planned. "I remember." My voice comes out husky, ragged.

His pupils dilate and his focus sharpens. He drops his head closer to mine. Our lips are inches away. "I liked what happened."

"Me, too," I whisper.

That's the last of either of our restraint. He wipes out all my insecurities by being completely and utterly resistible. His lips smash against mine and I throw my arms around his neck. Need rages inside me, and I ignore the alarm at the back of my mind that's trying to tell me this is crossing all boundaries and there's no going back.

My ability to be responsible around Simon is fatigued. I'm not strong enough to resist him.

Cool metal presses against my ass as he shoves my shorts down, but I don't think twice about it. My hands are busy yanking his bottoms past his sudden erection. He's hard for me this quickly and the satisfaction I feel is another balm for my hurt pride.

My shorts and underwear are tugged down and drop down my thighs to pool around my ankles. I don't have to step out of them. I'm being lifted. I cling tighter to Simon, my tongue clashing with his. We can't get enough of each other.

I automatically spread my legs for him and his thick length prods my entrance. He wedges a hand between us to steady himself and check that I'm ready, but it's a waste of time. I clench my legs to encourage him to just fucking thrust already.

He pushes in. One smooth jerk of his hips.

I moan against his mouth and he flattens a big hand on my thigh.

His unsteady breath wafts over my mouth. "God, Natalie. It's been too fucking long."

"I haven't been—" I gasp as he moves inside me. Nothing I could do on my own fills me like him. "I haven't done this since—" The ecstasy leaves me incoherent.

He pulls almost all the way out and shoves back in. I tighten my legs around him.

He kisses down my chin to my neck. "There's only been you. Just you."

The confirmation that he hasn't been with anyone else is gasoline poured directly on the burning fire of my desire. He plants open-mouth kisses along my neck and works my shirt up between us.

I have to prop my hands on the washer. My chest is bared, and he lavishes attention on my breasts over the material of my bra, all the while steadily thrusting.

"I'm not going to last long." He switches to the other nipple. They're straining against the fabric, sensitive to the point of exquisite pain and the only remedy is his touch. "You feel too fucking good."

I arch into him. He's always been able to get me off with little effort. It's one reason why I haven't touched myself since we divorced. The work of getting myself to orgasm when he can do it with a tilt of his head and a few flicks of his tongue just increases my tension instead of relieving it.

He changes the angle, knowing exactly how I like it when we do it standing up. His blunt tip hits the right spot over and over and over until I'm shaking.

I throw my arms around him and he straightens so I can bury my face in his neck to muffle my cries. Despite my efforts, noise escapes in a series of squeaks, panting, and low moans as I come all over him.

"God, Natalie. You kill me." He jacks his hips to impale me once more and stiffens. I look up to see the rigid clench of his jaw and how he's throwing his head back to ride out his climax. I hold him as he releases inside of me.

I'm still on the pill. It was on a list of decisions I didn't want to make when our marriage imploded. I knew full well I wouldn't be needing it because moving on with someone else was the last thing on my mind. Yet, hoping for Simon to show up at the door begging for a reconciliation was a dream I wasn't prepared to give up at the time.

Today, I'm grateful for the decision. Adding a baby to this uncertain time would only complicate matters and put more pressure on Simon when he's only just committed to making a change.

We cling to each other. My face is turned so I'm staring at the wall with the light switch. The machine hums under me, letting me know that I can't get enough of this man. He could haul me off to bed and I'd gladly stay there, getting pleasured by him, like all the times we used to before we had kids.

His grip on me loosens and he's pulling away when we hear Abby call, "Mom? Dad?"

* * *

Simon

Natalie's a ninja at avoiding me when we're still under the same roof.

After our frantic redressing to keep from getting busted half-naked by Abby, she left the laundry room to check on the kids and I stayed to get my body under control. I didn't miss her flushed cheeks and the sense of loss that played out on her face when I pulled out of her.

I don't regret what happened, but I regret that we didn't have a chance to talk about it. It wasn't just a quick fuck. Sleeping with Natalie was never about fleeting pleasure. Every time I'm with her is a commitment to us. I've never looked into love languages, but if there's one that involves sex, then that's mine.

I know it's the same with her. The similarity was a small part of the magnet that drew us together in Business 101. I had no interest in getting distracted from my studies by parties and random hookups. Wharton wasn't cheap for my parents, who liked to pretend it was in their social circle. And I liked sex as much as the next guy, but I could never disentangle it from emotions that a young, single guy like me wasn't supposed to have.

As soon as I laid eyes on Natalie, I sensed she was the same. Not a prude, but with hard boundaries when it came to how she allowed herself to be treated. Somehow, I pushed past those limits last year and it ended our marriage.

But I'm doing better. I've been around for her and for the kids and I'm still getting my job done.

We can do this. I just have to convince her of that.

I get a modest supper of macaroni and cheese and peas ready. Something easy on the kids' stomachs. Natalie is working in the office, but I suspect she's hiding. Abby tried to play outside but slogged back in after fifteen minutes. They're low on energy, but I'm sure they'll be back to normal tomorrow.

While the girls are eating, Natalie comes out, makes herself a plate and disappears. She does it while I'm on the back deck on the phone. Helena's been a champ fielding any calls and messages left by clients over the weekend, but I check in with both her and Charlie.

Inside, Natalie stays hidden and I get the girls ready for bed. She emerges to tuck them in and read stories. When she leaves their bedroom, I'm waiting, my arms folded across my chest, at the bottom of the stairs. There's no way she can miss me.

She stops, anxiety darkening her gaze and she chews on her lower lip. "I guess we need to talk."

Finally. I wave toward the couch. The living room is as public as we can get and if we talk in hushed tones, the kids won't hear.

She chooses the recliner and my right eye twitches. She's making sure I can't sit in the same space as her.

I pick the end of the couch closest to her. Not because I want to be confrontational. I crave being close to her and I have over seven months to make up for. Actually nine from when I moved out and divorce proceedings started.

"About earlier—" she started.

"I loved every minute of it." I don't mean to interrupt her, but I get the feeling that if I let her talk, she'll talk herself out of any progress our washing machine sexcapade made. "And I love you, Natalie. I've never quit loving you."

Alarm flashes in her eyes and she shrinks in the chair. I came on too strong.

"Sorry." I hold my hands out like I'm showing her I'm unarmed. "I just wanted it out there. I'm trying. I want to be the man you need and want in your life."

"You are, but your work always comes first."

"We both know how important it is to me. But I'm trying to balance it."

She folds her lips in and looks away. I wait, hoping she'll give me a peek into what's going on in that pretty head of hers. Surprisingly, she talks. "Why didn't you try before?"

"Before what?"

"The divorce." She looks me square in the eye and the weight of my answer lands on my shoulders.

The answer isn't as hard as she must assume. "You were miserable. I'll do anything to make you happy, even end our marriage."

Shock flickers in her eyes and she huffs out a laugh. "I thought you couldn't be bothered by the matter and signed the papers so you could get back to work."

"With you gone, I have nothing but work."

"You had nothing but work before I was gone."

I'm starting to see where she's coming from. A weekend like last weekend, I would've flown out and she would've been alone. Natalie was a powerhouse at the job. But we'd become more coworkers who had sex and less husband and wife. I didn't hire Helena until Natalie backed out of the job entirely. And I had to hire Charlie then too.

"I want to be better," I confess. Just like I tried to be a better son and a brother to be proud of, I want to be the husband of her dreams and a father who can provide his kids with the world. "Can you give me a chance?"

I'll get on my damn knees and beg. I want my family back.

She rests her head in her hand and rocks in the chair. "What would we tell the girls? My parents? What if it doesn't work out?"

There's no easy answer and I don't rush mine. It'll work. There's no other option. "We'll start slow. Like we have been."

She frowns. "What happened earlier was not slow."

I bite back a comment about my quick performance. Now's not the time for levity. Besides, I was always as fast or as slow as she needed, including today. "Since that first kiss in your office, we've been building to this point." It was earlier than that kiss. When I walked in on her after her shower. That was my moment of clarity. When I knew I would fight to get my wife back. I would find a way to make her happy being married to me.

"Still, that was only three weeks ago."

"We can keep it between us if that makes you more comfortable."

She dips her head. "No kissing in front of the girls. No comments about getting back together."

My hopes soar. She's willing to try it. I was afraid I had missed my chance. But she's giving me one. "When... how..." I spread my hands. "So we can't actually go on dates and stuff?"

She looks around and her gaze sticks on the stairs leading to the guest bedroom. "We should keep things the way they are." My hopes crash. The last thing I want to do is go back to my empty, boring condo. "But on the nights you get them, you can stay here. In the guest room."

I know what she's doing. She's keeping distance between us, giving herself an out. If I can't prove I've changed, it's an easy change back to the way things were and no one else knows we tried and failed.

"Okay." I rise and hold out my hand.

She eyes it like I'm holding a poisoned apple, but she slips her hand in mine and stands.

I tug her close. "Technically, that means I should go home until Wednesday night. But the girls are in bed and they're not even talking to each other. Take me to your room, Natalie. I need to reconnect."

Her breath hitches and her gaze flicks from the stairs to across the house toward her bedroom. Her nod is slight but perceptible.

My body ignites and all the fantasies from the last eight-plus months of abstinence vie for attention. I plan to live them all out as long as she's willing.

We enter her bedroom and she shuts the door and locks it.

Yes.

Thirteen

Simon

My entire body clenches. This isn't a quickie in the laundry room. It's a chance for me to make love to my wife, to show her how she's the center of my world and that everything I do is for her and our kids.

I could strip her down, lay her out, and have my way with her, but— No, that's what I'm going to do. Only I'm not going to rush it. Every time she wants to hide in that pretty head of hers, I'm going to make her want to be present—with me.

We could get interrupted. The girls could call out, one could be sick again. There could be a number of things that happen to stop us, so I'll seize each second.

She stops at the edge of the bed and trails her fingers over the rumpled bedding.

I go for a little levity only because I sense that if I come on too strong, she's going to add to that wall she's built between me and her. "Still don't make the bed in the mornings, I see?"

She looks at me over her shoulder with a faint smile. "It'll just get messy again."

Her standard response emboldens me. Everything has changed between us, but at the same time, nothing has. We're just two kids who met in college and decided to do this thing called life together. Our path took a detour, but we can get back on it.

I position myself behind her and brush my hands over her shoulders, down her arms, until I can thread my fingers with hers. Burying my nose in her hair, I inhale the familiar scent. I never paid attention to what shampoo she bought, the same stuff I used to use. I'm dependent on whatever Charlie orders for delivery and that explains why I start the day with an emptiness. I have nothing of her in my condo, not even her lingering scent. Only memories.

"Simon..." There's a hitch in her voice. She's retreating into her head.

"Natalie. Stay with me. Stay right here with me in this moment. I don't have a right to ask, but I'm begging you now."

"You're not down on your knees." She ends her joke with a strangled gasp. I know her well enough to guess that she didn't catch the innuendo before she said it.

A sly smile lifts my lips and I ease to my knees.

She stiffens and sidles to the side, releasing my hands. "Oh. No, um... I haven't cleaned up since... I mean."

I don't fucking care, but it bothers her and I'll take care of it. Rising, I grab a hand and draw her along with me to the bathroom. "If you insist on being clean, then allow me to help."

I flip on the bathroom light because I don't want to miss an inch of her creamy, freckled skin.

"Do we need the light?" She avoids looking at herself in the mirror while I flip the shower on. Six heads send water cascading in all directions.

"Strip down, Natalie." I never give her a direct order and she blinks at me. But I don't miss the desire clouding her bright eyes.

She rolls her shirt up and over her head, dropping it on the floor. Next is her shorts. She hesitates at her bra, but I arch a brow. Her scowl is only partly playful as she unhooks it.

Yes.

I've missed those breasts. Unlike that time I walked in on her, I'm going to get to touch them. She wiggles out of her underwear, those delicious mounds swaying.

Finally, she's naked and I'm allowed to look my fill.

Her gaze lifts behind me to the shower. "I'll do my business in the shower while you undress."

Heat rolls out of the shower enclosure. It's ready for her. I don't care to push her too far past her comfort zone. And as much as I like shower sex, I want to be with Natalie in a bed. *My* bed.

I step aside. She has to pass me to get into the shower. I stop her before she enters by grazing her chin with the backs of my fingers. "I'll have a towel waiting for you." *Don't take too long.*

She nods, a soft smile gracing her pink lips. While she cleans up, I get our towels ready and undress. I pick up our dirty clothes so there's one less thing to distract her.

"Can I come in?" I call quietly.

She appears at the edge of the ceramic tile wall that blocks the shower from the rest of the bathroom. "Yes, I'm done."

My body gets the fastest wash of its life while she towels off. She's finished when I step out. The fluffy blue-topaz towel's wrapped around her and she's bent over a drawer, selecting a comb.

"Here. Let me." I dry off in record time but don't bother slinging the towel around my waist. My erection would prevent it from staying.

I take the comb from her hand and stand behind her so we're both looking into the mirror. Her uncertainty is scrawled across her face. Instead of letting it deter me, I use it to strengthen my resolve. This is going to be a journey for both of us.

Gently, I comb through her damp curls. "Want a braid?"

"Just a basic one so the sheets don't get soaked."

It doesn't take me long, but as she relaxes into my touch, I prolong the task. She's always liked when I take care of her hair. It requires more time, sometimes more than she has.

When was the last time I did this for her? For the girls?

She catches my frown. "Is everything okay?"

"Just trying to remember the last time I did this."

"It's been a while," she says quietly. Our gazes connect in the mirror.

"I feel like I've been thinking that about a lot of stuff."

She doesn't comment and it's probably best. There's nothing she can say that won't drive the point home more. Just because I lived here didn't mean I was around.

I divide her hair into three sections and braid it. She produces a tie.

All done.

Our gazes meet in the glass again. It'd be so easy to reach around and unlatch the flap of fabric holding her towel in place. But I don't.

"Drop the towel, Natalie."

* * *

Natalie

If we do this, there's no going back. I can't write it off as a frantic, impulsive coupling against the washing machine. I can't use the overtired, overwrought and overemotional excuse. I'm all of those things, but he's giving me plenty of time to back out.

That's the last thing I want to do.

I unhook the towel and let it fall to our feet. There's no more fabric between us. His hot erection brands my back but moves away when he leans over to press tiny kisses along my shoulder up to my neck.

A shiver traces down my body. I close my eyes and enjoy the sensation and not having to rush.

He reaches around me and cups my breasts. His warm, strong grip cradles me, sapping the rest of my inhibitions despite how this will complicate things.

Things are officially complicated, but we've decided to go through it together.

Together. Like we are now.

I flutter my eyes open and roll my head to the side, making room for him to nibble his way up my neck.

A blush graces my skin from my cheeks down my torso. I'm usually cold after a shower, constantly moving to keep warm. But not tonight. He's a furnace at my back that won't let one goose bump through unless he's the cause of it.

Seeing him through the mirror isn't enough. "Take me to the bed."

He looks up, his lips still pressed against my skin. I don't know what he's searching for. To see if I'm copping out? Too self-conscious?

It's neither. I want to hold him like I've been dreaming of doing for months. I want to not go to bed alone for once.

Sensing my resolution, he leads me to bed. I sit and scoot back, drawing him over me. His weight is better than any blanket. I widen my legs until he fits in the cradle of my thighs, but he doesn't do more than kiss me. Slow, languid, exploring. Our tongues caress against each other. Our hands roam of their own free will. I stroke mine up and down his back, around his sides, then up and across his shoulders. Familiar planes of muscle ripple under my hands.

He shifts to nibble his way down. Down my neck, over my chest, across my belly, only to pause and look up. "I've been dreaming about this every damn night. It's kept me awake for hours," he says hoarsely.

I haven't been the only one. I wondered. I hoped. To hear it confirmed makes me certain that moving forward is the right thing to do. Because at the end of our marriage, he didn't act like a man who'd lose sleep over losing me.

"Simon, I didn't think..." He drops a kiss right at my bikini line. I suck in a breath and arch my back.

"Didn't think what?" His warm breath wafts over my fevered skin.

I didn't think he loved me anymore. "I thought you were over me before I was over you," is all I can say.

"I'd never get over you." Another kiss, lower this time. "Not in a thousand years." He flicks his tongue across my clit, a shot of pleasure jacks my hips up. "When you kissed me in the office, I knew we still had a chance."

He was the only one then. But now? I think we have a chance too.

Just like our kiss after we landed on the bed, Simon takes his time. He's an expert when it comes to my body and he proves that he hasn't forgotten a thing.

Exquisite pleasure builds, a rolling thunderstorm before

the torrent is released. I twist the sheets until one edge jerks free of the mattress and lightning explodes across my vision.

"Simon!" I manage to temper my volume at the last second to keep from waking the kids. Ecstasy cascades over me as Simon carries me over the edge and far past it.

He doesn't surge up right away after I'm done. His lips feather across one thigh, then the other, before he leisurely makes his way back up my body.

I widen my legs, ready to have him inside. But he pauses over me, his weight held off me.

"Remember the time in my dorm?"

We had sex a lot in the dorms, but I know exactly which time he's talking about. We'd just started sleeping together and went at it as often as possible. He was nothing like my clunky high school boyfriend. Simon studied my body as thoroughly as he prepared for exams—long hours for as many days as possible.

One time, we fell asleep, spooned together in a little twin bed. When we woke, he rolled me on my side, with my top leg higher, and we had sex. That position hit all the right spots at the right times in a way that hadn't happened before. I went wild, bucking against him, and we broke the box spring. I used my birthday money to help replace it.

After that, our cost-conscious selves were cautious about using the position.

"We know this bed can take it," I reply.

He puts me in the same position and pushes in. Our groans mingle. There's nothing like being filled by my husband.

This isn't like the rest of the night has been. He doesn't take his time. Thrust after thrust, he stokes my pleasure like only he knows how. Like only he'll ever know how until I crest again and press my face into the mattress to muffle my cries.

He jerks his hips and grinds out my name as he comes. The only downside to this position is that I can't hold him while he climaxes. But once he's done, he withdraws and collapses next to me, curling me into him.

"The bed's a mess," he mumbles.

I giggle. "Good thing we took our showers first."

"Solid planning, Mrs. Underwood."

My smile wavers. I thought of him as my husband, but the ex part is still there. Yet, I don't want to rain melancholy on this moment. "Good thing you're here, Mr. Underwood."

I wiggle away from him, dip into the bathroom and clean up. By the time I'm done, the bed is made. He has a towel slung around his hips and an apologetic smile.

He scratches the back of his neck. "I, uh, don't want to go, but…"

"The girls." Finding him in bed with me would make them ask harder questions.

He nods and drifts closer. Tipping my chin up, he gives me a sweet good-night kiss. "Sleep tight, Natalie."

"Good night, Simon."

He leaves the door open when he goes. We never wanted to be closed off from the girls with their rooms across the house. Tonight, I don't want to be shut off from Simon.

Soon. If things keep going this well, he'll be going to bed with me every night again—and if he's really changing his ways, it'll stay that way.

Fourteen

Natalie

The agreed-upon arrangement regarding Simon staying at the house lasted one whole week before Wednesday nights and every other weekend turned into him staying at the house every night.

I can't complain.

He's usually home by the time I have to tuck the girls in, and he's kept his Wednesday workload from encroaching on his normally scheduled night with the girls and I've been able to keep my personal training appointments.

Once the girls are tucked in, I get almost no work done. Simon and I sneak everywhere in the house where we can close and lock a door. The sex is off the charts. I wake up sore in the mornings from whatever position he bent me over in the night before.

I puff my hair out of my face.

It's Friday and the Fourth of July is on Monday. My

parents are messaging me about our plans and whether we want to go over there for the day.

I haven't told them about Simon yet. The girls talk about him, but haven't mentioned that their dad's staying with us full time. I think Mom and Dad suspect something's changed in our postdivorce schedule.

Simon's not home from work yet and I just kicked the girls outside. I slip onto the deck, relax in a lounge chair and contemplate my phone.

With a resigned sigh, I call Dad.

Dad answers with, "I don't want to be a pest, but the Burkhardts invited us over and your mom and I don't really want to go, but she feels like crap lying, so we're hoping you can throw us a preserver and save us from a night of listening to Benji talk about his lake cabin and how awesome it is and then try to sell it to me all night."

The Burkhardts have been my parents' neighbors for five years. They call themselves snowbirds, but they never go south during the winter, nor do they visit their lake cabin in the summer. However, they have time-shares in both places and will block you in a corner to tell you about it.

"Tell Mom her conscience can be clean. You guys can even come over here so you don't feel like you have to invite them over when they peer over the fence."

"You're my favorite kid."

"I'm an only child, so I hope so." I gaze at the girls playing. Even if Simon goes to work on Monday, his athletic shoes will be at the door and his hoodie is hanging up in the mudroom. The guest room bed is always neatly made, but the drawers are full and the closet has his suits. Last Sunday, he ran back to the condo to refresh his weekly suit supply. He's incorporating into our lives.

"Want us to bring anything?"

"Just yourselves and whatever goodies Mom's going to spoil the girls with. Um, Dad…"

"Uh-oh." He knows my tone. He guessed I was pregnant with Abby my junior year of college by how I greeted him when I called.

"It's about Simon."

"Do I even wanna know?" He's partly joking, but I know he cares for Simon too.

"Remember when you said kick him out or move him in? It seems that I picked moving him in."

Stunned silence is my reply. A few moments pass. "Do I even want to know?" he says again.

"We're taking it slow."

"Nat. He's living there."

"I know. I mean, he's in the guest room and we haven't told the girls that we're trying to work things out. He's been doing a lot better juggling work and homelife, but…"

"But what, kiddo?"

I rub my forehead. "But it's Simon."

"He hasn't been hiding who he is. Here. You tell your mother."

I chew the inside of my lip while he hands the phone to Mom.

"Is everything okay?" she asks.

I go straight for the news. "Simon and I are trying to work things out."

"That's… good?"

"I hope so." Well, so much for a resounding yes.

She hears everything I haven't said but spoke about enough last year. "Are you happy, honey?"

I would be ecstatic, but the underlying anxiety won't go away. "It's been a month and he's been around more than he was for years before we split."

"Okay. That's a start."

"We're taking it slow, but he's living here."

A disgruntled noise drifts over the line. "He's living there?"

"It's easier that way."

"For now, maybe." She fielded a lot of grandkid time when I was meeting with lawyers and signing papers. And provided a shoulder when I broke down in her bathroom, smelling like chopped onion and salsa, and told her my decision. "Well, you two are adults, and you've both been reasonable so far. I just... I just hope that he's really seen the light and knows what's on the line."

The sliding door opens and Simon steps out. His suit jacket is off and his tie is long gone. His sleeves are rolled up his forearms and he's holding a couple of longnecks.

"Me too." I accept the drink, warmth washing over me that we're slipping into a routine I love and have missed for so long. "I'll let you go, Mom. We'll see you Monday."

I hang up. Simon's stretched out in the lounge chair next to me. His trousers are tight around his thighs and hips. He takes a leisurely pull off his bottle, his abs flat and his steely gaze sweeping across the lawn.

I can't wait for tonight when I get him all to myself. "How was your day?"

"Busy." His focus switches to me and his eyes heat as he takes me in. I'm not wearing anything more than a dab of mascara that's probably worn off and a narrow pink headband to keep my curls off my face. The wind stirs them up, but not enough that I have to bind them entirely.

But the way Simon looks at me makes me feel like I'm wearing an evening gown that compliments my curves instead of exaggerating them when, instead, I have on pink fabric shorts that match my headband and an old white T-shirt.

"How was your day?" He's sincere.

"Good. Errands and stuff. Nothing earth-shattering."

"That's always nice."

While he was at work, managing millions and millions of his clients' dollars and networking with the firms he invests in, I was running to Target, the grocery store, and taking the car in for an oil change. The afternoon was full of putting groceries away and quiet time for all of us. What I did was nothing like what Simon does all day. But he's never treated me like I'm lesser for it.

I have friends who stay home and their spouse makes only a fraction of what Simon brings in, but they act like they get to dictate everything that happens in the home while claiming they don't have to lift a finger because that's the job of the person at home.

Simon considers us partners. It's why it hurt so much when it seemed like he forgot about us entirely when he assumed that his job was critical to keep our homelife the way it was.

I love our house, but if his job went through some tough years, I'd downsize in a heartbeat. As long as we're all together. But Simon refuses to go backward in life and that includes keeping everything we worked for. I hope his bachelorhood is firmly in the past.

He shifts in his chair and sets his beer down. The glass clinks ominously on the top of the patio table. "I, uh, got a request for an interview. A few actually."

"For what?"

"That article."

Oh. Hatred sweeps through my veins like a summer drought, turning all my warm fuzzies into tinder. Simon and I are working on us. Why do I still hate that article and any reference to it?

Because he's not eligible. He's mine.

My hand tightens around my own beer. If I set it down,

I might crack it or the table. "What do they want to talk to you about?"

"Probably another interest piece. Word of it made the rounds and the local news wants to talk to me and a few of the local magazines would like a feature." The corners of his jaw flex. "I can't say no. It'd look bad for business. But I have to know what I can say. About us."

* * *

Simon

I play it cool, waiting for her answer. My fingers are folded across my stomach to keep from fidgeting and I keep the hopeful tone out of my voice.

I act like I'm negotiating a contract.

Comparing my marriage to boardroom discussions leaves a sour taste in my mouth, but I also recognize how fragile our relationship is at this point.

"Us?" Natalie looks away, her expression deep in thought. "Why would we be any of their business?"

"Because my single status was the point of the whole article." That and my wallet. I should've never done it. Helena had a point about the free advertisement and getting my name out there to a new audience.

I'm at the precipice of cashing in on that fame. I've already accepted the interviews because I'd look like an elitist ass who didn't help local entrepreneurs. I stock their magazines in my office and page through them on my way out the door. This is my chance to do more for them while also getting Underwood Equity in front of potential clients or promising companies seeking investors.

"I don't know," she finally says. "I just told Mom and Dad. Do you think we're ready to tell the whole world?"

"It'd only be the Fargo viewing area."

She rolled her eyes toward me. "The girls don't even know."

"We can talk to them."

"They're too young to understand," she says in a definitive tone.

Don't I get a say? "I don't think they are."

"You weren't the one answering questions about why you weren't here. Or why you weren't around Christmas morning. You weren't drying their terrified tears when they thought there were monsters in their room, but you weren't here to save them."

Her points were each heartbreaking, but she's forgetting one thing. I sit forward, my elbows on my legs. My voice shakes with repressed emotion. "I had my own times when I was calming them in the middle of the night because they're in a new place and you're not there. They've cried on my shoulder about us being apart too."

Fleeting emotions run through Natalie's face. She's not used to me getting this heated in a discussion, not toward her. But talking to me like I don't know my own kids hit on a sensitive spot I haven't inspected in a long time.

Natalie, Abby, and Maddy are my life. Yeah, I'm gone a lot, working hard for them. But I do the best I can to keep up on their lives. To be present when I'm around. I heard Natalie's complaints of how much I was gone and I'm working on that.

She gets up and disappears into the house. I glance at the backyard. Maddy's in the sandbox and Abby is on the swing, each in their own world.

I go after Natalie. She's at the counter. Her hands are

pressed on the top and she's glowering at the surface. Even though we're on the brink of a fight, I still take a moment to admire the curves of her legs. My blood warms, reminding me to tread carefully or my days worshiping that body will be limited.

"I didn't mean to get so upset." I learned the art of *I'm always wrong* early. I can credit years of my own parents arguing and wondering why my father didn't step back and admit that he was in the wrong once in a while. The ol' Underwood pride. "I understand what you're saying."

She huffs out a breath. "It's one thing to understand but another to actually get it. *They* have to come first."

Telling Natalie that I understand used to mollify her before. But saying it when I didn't feel it led us to this point. I have to prove I get it, or this argument could have me packing my bags, something I never want to do again. "Then I'll play off the eligible bachelor bit and try to change the subject."

Displeasure ripples over her face. I feel the same way. I have no issues going on TV and putting in print that I'm trying to win back my wife. But if she wants a buffer between the world and us, then I'll give it to her.

"They're going to be tenacious." She waves her hand to me. "I mean, look at you."

Seeing my chance to dissolve the tension between us, I swagger over. "You think I'm good-looking."

Her scowl is only partly playful. "It's why you get away with so much."

I'm briefly taken aback. "So much what?"

"Moving in? Sneaking into my bedroom each night." She drops her voice to a whisper. "My office."

Taking her on her desk the other night is an especially fond memory. It was the first time we'd done it in that room. "I believe you were the one that made the first move."

A smile plays over her lips. "My parents are coming over on the Fourth. Want to do hamburgers and hot dogs?"

"Absolutely." Since her parents know about us and are willing to come hang out when I'm here, maybe they'd be open to watching their grandkids for a date night Sunday evening before the Fourth.

I can't gather Natalie into my arms. We're right in front of the window and I respect her desire to keep our rekindling private.

Natalie licks her lower lip, making it hard to stick to my good intentions. "You really think all they're going to care about is that you're single?"

"If they think I'm ready to mingle, yes." I peek outside to make sure I'm clear and give her a quick kiss on the forehead. "I'll take care of it."

"You shouldn't have to."

I lift a shoulder. "I did that stupid interview. I have to pay the consequences."

"It…" She wrinkles her nose. "It was a good piece. Tasteful, surprisingly."

"I got a few extra clients. I was afraid it'd scare the companies I wanted to invest with, but it was good publicity. They either don't pay attention or don't care since I was shown in a good light."

"Helena has good instincts."

"She does." I think back to the last month. "She's been… different the last few weeks."

Natalie busies herself, getting out the supplies for sub sandwiches. "How do you mean?"

"More professional. Distant. It's not like she's an ass-kisser, but she's definitely cooler toward me."

"Well, you have been handing off a lot more duties with little warning. Maybe it's interfering with her own life."

"I don't know anything about her life. But she can

always say something." I tilt my head to admire Natalie's ass while she's digging in the fridge.

She backs out and tosses a bag of farmers' market lettuce by the buns. "She's probably not comfortable pointing out that the demands of her job have changed, but the pay hasn't. Or that the extra work interferes with her homelife."

"I'm not a bad boss. Why wouldn't she be willing to talk to me about her position?"

"Just because you would have no problem shooting the breeze with your boss before transitioning into your opinion on work and how much you're paid doesn't mean everyone is like that."

She's referring to the time in college when I turned a nonpaid intern position into one with a decent hourly wage. I think about her point and make a mental note to talk to Helena when we get back in the office next week. Maybe I should check in with Charlie too.

When she breezes by me, I snag her arm and gently pull her in. "Thank you."

She tilts her head back. "For what?"

"You make me a better man. A better boss."

She softens under me and I go in for a kiss. Giggles at the sliding door precede the whoosh of it opening.

Natalie stiffens and spins around to grab the silverware for tonight. I let a beat of disappointment hit me in the chest before reaching over her to get the plates.

"Mom, guess what?" Abby's grin widens. "Dad! Guess what?"

Maddy crowds around her. "She can flip."

Natalie's brow rises. Sometimes these guessing games aren't nearly as exciting for us. "Flip over what?"

"Off the back of the swing," Abby answers. "Watch."

Our supper planning is paused as we go out to watch. All I can think about—other than hoping Abby's flip is as innocent as skipping across soft grass and not something that gives me an early heart attack—is how fast Natalie pulled away.

She's really afraid the girls will find out. To me, that means she lacks confidence in us.

I'm going to change her mind. And I'll recruit her parents to give us a date night to do it.

Fifteen

Simon

Natalie fidgets with the menu, flipping it back and forth. She's uncomfortable and I start to doubt myself. I made reservations at one of the few fine dining places open on a Sunday. The girls are sleeping at Natalie's parents' and will come home tomorrow at lunch.

Her nerves bring back memories.

The year before we were going to graduate college, Natalie showed up on my apartment doorstep, her eyes full of tears, and told me that she was pregnant.

We'd been dating nearly two years by then and had our future planned out. Her feelings had streamed across her face along with her tears. She'd thought she'd lose me. She thought our hopes and dreams would radically change.

Her family was waiting to move to where we ended up, but she thought she'd be moving back in with her parents and trying to finish her degree online. Each tear that had streaked down her face was evidence that she thought I'd rocket out and live my best life, sending her and the kid a little money here and there.

I wasn't worried. That night, I looked at the girl I fell head over heels for and thought about the ring burning in my pocket. I'd wait to propose until she knew I was doing it for her and not because she was pregnant.

I'd pulled her into my arms, told her everything was going to be all right and between me and her parents, we'd get through school—together. My own parents thought I was insane, but I didn't miss their lack of surprise. It was a given that I wouldn't live up to my brother. Ever.

Those years had been hard, but some of our best ones. They laid a thick foundation that I never thought would fracture.

But it did. And tonight, I have to convince Natalie once more that divorce is only a bump in the road. No, that's not right. It's like the arrival of Abby. An event that puts out signs of where our life is going. We don't have to change course if we don't want to.

"Everything's so... adult," she whispers.

This is supposed to be a fun evening. We couldn't afford places like this when we were a young couple with small kids. By the time we could, we just didn't. Natalie would probably say it was because I was working all the time, and yes, that had something to do with it.

I think we forgot to make us a priority. We still aren't and Natalie won't change her mind. The girls come first.

"They serve the same food you buy at the farmers' market." The big draw of the place is how it sources most of its ingredients locally.

"I guess. But I'm at the farmers' market in sweats and Nikes."

Her curls are styled tonight. Less frenzied. I like frenzied, but I also like polished Natalie. She's wearing a sundress and a gauzy cardigan to cover her shoulders. I look like I stepped right out of the office, except I left the suit jacket at home.

Truthfully, I hated putting even this on. My time back at home and handing more work over to Helena has given me a new appreciation for casual wear. Summer is not the time for suits and in the frigid winter, I'd rather dress in a nice warm parka from North Face and wear a stocking hat. And boots. I miss shoes that actually keep my feet warm.

I shake off the thought. I work hard. Dress for the job you want. Being a dad isn't a job. But I like the uniform.

Natalie orders a pasta dish and I choose the walleye with green tomato salsa.

"It's not macaroni and cheese, is it?" she says wryly.

She's relaxing and I commit to taking her on more of these dates. To remind her that she's an adult with her own needs and, soon, a business owner.

"How's the training going? For the half-marathon," I ask. She's usually down in the gym when I leave for work. I only stopped once to tell her goodbye. She seemed flustered. I interrupted her groove.

"Good. I meet Aleah twice a week and I've been getting in the extra runs on my own. She helped me work out the schedule, so I get tomorrow off." Her smile is sheepish. "I never thought I'd be a runner."

"Why not?"

She gives me a look like I should know why. By college, she was into classes and loved going on walks, but I never saw her as the nonathlete that she classified herself as. "I never played sports."

"Doesn't mean you can't."

"Speaking of which, don't be surprised when Abby asks if you can coach her soccer team this fall."

I'm interested. I used to help coach in high school. The

energy of little kids is like nothing else. Going back to the basics, when it's just fun to play and not stress about the outcome, is a treat.

I'd love to coach again. When I talk to Helena, I'll have to talk to her about opening my schedule this fall so I can. To do that, we'll have to hire another person. That's on my mental to-do list for next week.

Natalie sips her water. "I tried to tell her that you might be too busy—"

"No. I'll see what I can do."

"But then Maddy is starting this year and will want you to coach too."

"I can make it work." I'll really have to talk with Helena. We'll definitely need another assistant, but also someone to work with client portfolios so I can concentrate on the equities side. My clients don't trust just anyone and many of them started with me when it was me and Natalie. We were a family business, but we promised and delivered the same outcome as if they invested with firms that wouldn't even let them close to anyone in the big office.

If I start doling out all my duties to Helena and another assistant, it wouldn't be the same company we started. Which is unrealistic. We're growing, serving more people, and we need the staff to do it.

"You'll coach both teams?"

Hearing the disbelief in her voice firms my resolve. "I'll make it work."

She sits back. The server fills our water glasses, giving us a break from conversing.

After the woman leaves, Natalie asks, "You'll really do that?"

"I want to be involved in their lives. Can you send Charlie the dates of the open houses at the school? I don't want to miss those. Especially not kindergarten."

Her brows lift higher. I've really caught her off guard. This shouldn't be so shocking. I was with her when Abby started kindergarten. I had to run out early, but I made it.

"Yeah, sure. I'll do that." Her entire being lightens as if she's come to a decision about me and the real likelihood that we'll make it. "What else do you have planned for a Sunday night date?"

"Down the street, there's an open mic night."

"We've never done one of those. *I've* never done one of those."

Did she think I cut loose when the ink was dried on our divorce papers? "If you haven't done it, then I haven't."

She ponders me for a few moments and I feel like a bug under a magnifying glass. "You said..." She bites her lower lip. "You said you hadn't slept with anyone after we split. Didn't you date at all?"

I meant it when I said there was only her. "Why would I?"

"You read the article. I'm sure you were asked."

"I was at work or at the condo. If I traveled, it was for business. Charlie took care of the meals, so I hardly had to go to the grocery store. If anything wasn't work related, I was with the kids."

"You had to have gotten hit on."

"Maybe. I didn't notice."

Her lips twist. "You never did."

It's my turn to study her. "I always had the feeling you thought I was one foot out the door." That feeling hasn't changed.

"What do you mean?"

The little crease in her forehead tells me she knows exactly what I mean. "We've been together since we were nineteen. Earlier tonight, I was thinking about when you told me that you were pregnant and how you thought I was going to break up with you."

"I didn't..." She sighs. "You know how different we grew up. You were all jock and I was all girl in the corner with a book."

"I happen to like girls in corners with books." I wince and chuckle. "That sounded better in my head."

She smiles but fiddles with the edge of her napkin. "You're too good to be true, and when I finally accepted that you were legit and weren't going to be swayed by a piece of ass that promised nothing but a good time, your focus became work."

"And you know why," I say quietly.

"I don't care about a big house or money."

"I know." That's not how she grew up. How I grew up was different. There was a stark difference in what Hayes was provided versus me. Hayes got the newest and the best. I got the rest. His college was fully funded and I worked my ass off for the rowing scholarship, but I had to pick up the rest.

I'm determined not to do that with my family.

Natalie

The last open mic act wraps up and I clap, astonished at the amount of talent in our area.

"I never knew we had so many local singers and poets," I say to Simon as we rise and push in our chairs.

"Me either. We'll have to come here more often."

It was fun. This whole night was fun. I struggle to recall when we last went out, just the two of us. When Abby was little, maybe, but we didn't do much more than dinner and a movie.

We've lived in Fargo for seven years and don't know all it offers. The couple that we chatted with between open mic sets said they've gone to comedy nights, wine tastings, and local brewery hops.

I'm already planning another date night soon.

I guess that means I've lost some of my anxiety that Simon's going to revert to his old ways.

We walk out to the sidewalk toward Simon's car. His hand is on my back. It's more of a protective gesture than to steer me away from other patrons heading home for the night.

"So, what now?" I ask. It's a few minutes after ten.

"A quiet house?" He grins at me. Fading daylight casts shadows over his face, making him look like the superhero I thought he resembled when I first saw him. No one could be that ridiculously cute and nice and not have something to hide. "I thought that since tomorrow's going to be a late night, we should turn in early tonight."

"Good call. We're going to pay for a late night of fireworks on Tuesday morning."

"I promised them the best spot to watch."

"Where's that?"

"I don't know yet."

I grin the whole way home. My body's tingling because I know what's coming next. "They've been talking constantly about tomorrow. I think they're excited."

"I made the mistake of saying we might check out Bonanzaville."

"You're crazy." He has a full day planned that's going to wipe out not only the kids but us and my parents. But Bonanzaville will be fun. They put on a fireworks show, and while we're waiting, we can tour their historical museum and displays. The girls would love the old-time general store and Fargo's first schoolhouse. We always talked about going, but we haven't yet.

His phone pings a few times, but he ignores it while driving. No one else calls him but Helena and his clients. It's a holiday weekend.

But he doesn't only invest nationally.

My glow from the date fades the closer we get to home. Simon's checking his messages.

He's clueless to my change in mood, but I'm masking it like normal. I don't say anything. If this is going to work, I have to trust him and give him a chance to deal with it.

"I'm not tired," he says as we enter the house. "Feel up to a show?"

Cuddling in our movie room has a nice ring to it. "What are you in the mood for?"

"You pick. I'll run and change."

He'll change all right. And check his messages. But he's trying.

I don't need to change. There're blankets in the movie room if I get cold, but I plan to share more than body heat with my husb—with Simon.

Clicking through streaming services, I find a *Spider-Man* we haven't seen. We share a love of action movies and I will never go wrong with a superhero movie. A lot of action and a little bit of romance.

I assume he hasn't seen it. I heard, loudly from the girls, that there's nothing good to watch at his place and he claims not to have gone out.

You're it for me. You were always it for me.

He was so sincere when he said that. A satisfied quiver runs through my belly.

Several minutes go by and I tire of watching the same clip playing over and over while waiting to hit play. I back out of the movie and choose an Earth documentary to pass the time. We might be able to sleep in tomorrow, but it's still getting late.

Finally, I click the screen off, irritation slithering through me.

His fucking work struck again.

I knew it.

He's locked himself away. He might as well pack his damn bags while he's on his call. Our first date night in years and this is how it ends?

I'm stomping up the stairs when I stop. My heart is racing and rage pounds at my skull. All those old feelings of inadequacy and helplessness are assailing me. But they're from before. We aren't in the same place as we were a year ago.

What am I doing? Am I going to pound on his door and demand he hang up the phone? Am I going to go to bed and lock him out?

The first time work majorly interferes and I'm ready to bail.

I close my eyes and take a steadying breath. He's doing his part and I have to do more than issue ultimatums. We haven't been home an hour and I'm ready to toss in the towel.

We had a wonderful dinner. A nice evening listening to a variety of live music, and now we're home.

It's too late for a show, but I can get ready for bed. And I'll be there by the time he's done.

I shuck off my dress and strip the rest of my clothes off. Washing the product out of my hair, I hum to myself. The sound fools me into loosening up.

I let out a long breath and visualize my tension going with it. It'll be okay. He'll come to bed. If we don't have sex it's not the end of the world. Having Simon undisturbed from Friday night to Sunday night is an oddity, one I would gladly have regularly.

Shutting the water off, I step out of the ceramic enclave for my towel. There's a tall form leaning in the doorway, a navy-blue towel dangling from his hand.

I yelp and steady my hand on my heart. "Simon. You scared me."

The corner of his mouth tilts up. He's still in his slacks. The top button is undone and his shirt is half-untucked. A rogue lock of hair rests on his forehead. "I'm glad that you aren't used to men waiting for you when your shower's done."

For the first time, it occurs to me that he might've thought I had been out dating. I repress a shudder. I don't think waiting twenty years after the divorce would've given me enough time to be ready for that.

No one can compare to Simon.

I look him over one more time. He's not offering me the towel and his gaze is licking over my bare body. There's one hanging next to me, but I don't grab for it. Shadows linger in his eyes where there were none before. "Is everything okay?"

He lifts his gaze and I can see that, no, it's not. "I took care of it. A London company that's going public and that Underwood Equity was in consideration with has been accused of scamming their clients. Mr. Waterson found out about it first and is on a rampage, demanding to know if this is how I do business now."

Ugh. I never liked Mr. Waterson and his leering gaze. "That's bad."

"I think it's rumors, but it's going to hurt their stocks and they're going into emergency mode."

I'm surprised that Simon isn't quick to believe speculation. He diligently researches companies. Many of his trips were to meet with owners, investors, and CEOs and also those who used to do business with them. Simon doesn't play around with his money or anyone else's.

He tosses the towel on the counter and starts unbuttoning his shirt. "I had to make a quick action plan and send Helena a list, starting with drafting a letter to our clients. But I may have to regretfully bail on the company, rumors or not. My clients' best interest comes first."

"You won't get tomorrow off." His shirt's almost off and the planes of his abs never cease to steal my attention, but they aren't enough to stop my disappointment.

"I'll work on it in the morning. With her help, we'll make it through the Fourth. Tuesday will be hell, but I'll have an excuse to delay the interviews."

I hate to give up any of his time when he doesn't ever take a full day off, but it's better than nothing. It's more than he's given us on the last few years of holidays. I was right to step back and trust him. He and I are in this together.

He's coming closer. His shirt flutters to the floor. I barely remember what he said last. Oh yes. Rescheduling the interviews. "Right. Because you're so eligible."

"I am."

He crowds me into the shower enclave and turns on the six showerheads. His slacks are still on, making this whole encounter feel spontaneous and illicit. I jump at the first hit of cold water, but my body heat warms it faster than the water heater.

He dips his head down, his mouth hovering over mine, water dripping off his hair, and unzips his pants. "Want me to show you how eligible I am?"

Sixteen

Simon

I was up before my alarm this morning. Helena sent the draft before ten a.m. and I was on conference calls all morning.

Natalie encouraged me to commandeer her office. She's changed since our date. Not as guarded. I made love to her last night in the shower and again when we dried off and got into bed.

Spending the night in the same bed as my wife, under the covers with her, is the highlight of my year. I won't give up until I have it every night.

I didn't want to ruin it with an alarm. I kept it on vibrate, but it didn't matter. I was already awake, my mind racing with the tasks ahead.

Pulling out of investing with the London firm would be better done face to face, and as much as I shouldn't rush it, I have prior commitments. One is cutting fruits and vegetables for today's celebration and the other two are on their way over with their grandparents. If I can get through today, tackling what I need for work and living up to my promises for the "funnest day ever" will do more to show Natalie I'm serious than any date night.

"I regret to inform you that Gaineworth Equity can no longer work—"

"For heaven's sake, Simon. Have a think on it. News only broke yesterday." Mr. Mellon's been up the whole night, trying to get ahead of his crumbling empire that was once so promising.

I feel shitty, but it has to be done. "I wish you the best, Lan. I have no doubt you'll learn from this and come back stronger than ever."

There's only mild begging for me to reconsider before I manage to get off the phone with him. That felt like shit. My fingers twitch to call him back. No, I can't risk my company for his. Others are relying on me. But when I can, I'll help Mr. Mellon as much as I can.

Time to check in with Helena.

Her tone is brisk but hushed when she answers. "Yes, Mr. Underwood."

I rattle off my discussion with Mr. Mellon and what we need to do to communicate with our investors. "Can you draft another letter to investors regarding the final decision? I'll take a look and get it sent out today."

"Today?" Her tone is sharp. There's a rustle on the other end of the line and murmuring. Her husband?

"Yes. We have to act fast. You know how Mr. Waterson likes to test us. He knows too many of our other clients."

I used to be a lot like him. It's why I was so hesitant to hire someone after Natalie stepped back. But Hayes's money came with expectations from myself and my parents. *I can't believe he left you so much. What did he think you could do with it?*

"Certainly, Mr. Underwood." The phone shuffled again like she put her hand over the receiver. "I'll have it to you by three o'clock today."

We'd be at Bonanzaville by then and I'd have to edit on the phone among a throng of people. "I know it's asking a lot, but I need it by noon."

There's a moment of silence on the other end. "Noon."

It doesn't quite sound like a confirmation in that dull tone, but if she says she'll do it, then she'll do it.

"I appreciate it." Natalie's words from Friday come back to me. It's a holiday for Helena too. "Look, I know it's too late to help us out today, but when we return to the office, we need to get an ad out for a new assistant, one for you. And we should probably start looking for a new location."

Neither of us needs the extra work, but it's the growing pains that come with running a successful business.

"That would... that would help."

I hang up, considering her relieved reaction. Once again, Natalie's insight into the company and the people behind it is spot on.

My fingers are flying over the keyboard when I hear the delighted shouts of the girls. I save my progress and push back. Going out, I get tackled with hugs before the girls dart away. Their arms are loaded with new sidewalk chalk, containers of bubble solution, and wands to make bubbles as big as them.

Just like I used to, I cross to my mother-in-law and give her a peck on the cheek. "Nana. So glad you're feeling better."

"Thank you for giving Natalie a week to pamper me."

I shake Pete's hand. He's grinning and relief washes through me. Being accepted by my in-laws is as important as Natalie's approval. What I didn't get with my own parents, I got with Janie and Pete Wagner. For Christmas, I received flannel pajama pants and various flavors of jerky. Blissfully normal gifts that came with no expectations.

My parents make donations in my and the girls' name, which I'm absolutely fine with, except I wished they'd include Natalie. But other than a card indicating where and how much they gave, we get little else. No phone calls with warm wishes for the holiday season. Natalie sends school pictures and videos every year and they thank me, not her.

"How was your date night?" Pete asks, clapping me on the back. "Abby wanted to call you a million times, but I talked her out of it. Janie finally distracted them with lemonade and cookies."

Janie gives Pete a playful shove. "You weren't supposed to tell them that." She winks at me. "Just like he's not supposed to say that this was well after their bedtime."

I enjoy the play between the two. "You were just helping them practice staying up late to see the fireworks tonight."

Natalie appears at my side, looking more relaxed than I've seen her in a while. "Are you all done for the day?" she asks quietly as her parents head to the back deck.

Not even close. But I'm not missing a holiday with my family. "I'm free for now. What do you want me to prepare?"

I'm rewarded with a grateful smile. "I can help you."

In the kitchen, we busy ourselves with pulling out strawberries, blueberries, melons, and the standard carrots and celery, the only vegetables the girls regularly sample. My mind drifts back to the call this morning. I discreetly check the time. Helena should have the letter done soon. As long as I have my phone on me and can sneak away for ten minutes, I can do enough to mitigate any damage and head off any rumors before tomorrow.

I position myself to cut while she rinses and arranges dishes. "Are you sure you're done for the day?" she asks.

She knows me too well. "I have a little more to do, but this comes first. I also told her that we needed to start our preparations for expanding."

I slice into a carrot, but Natalie is silent. Peering over my shoulder, I start chuckling. She's staring at me from over her shoulder, disbelief in her eyes. "Expanding?"

"I told her that we'll start to look for a new space and work on hiring her own assistant. I think it's time. You need more help, and it's so nice to spend a holiday together."

There's a hint of wistfulness in her voice. "I feel like there's a but."

"Oh, it's nothing. I mean, I feel bad that Rachel has to do another holiday by herself. One of those things where I'm so happy we can be together, but then sad because not everyone has this opportunity."

"Then invite her."

She sets a colander full of ripe strawberries next to my cutting board and gazes up at me, guarded delight in her hazel eyes. "Really? You don't mind?"

"The more the merrier. We have plenty of food and she can bail before we go to Bonanzaville for fireworks, or she can join us, depending on how she and her kiddos feel." I want Natalie to keep the friendships she strengthened during our split. It wasn't until she talked about Aleah and Rachel that I reflected on our lack of couple friends and my lack of friends and acquaintances outside of work.

When Abby was a toddler and we'd go to the park, I'd strike up conversations with other dads, but it never went far. I always had to return to work.

"You're okay with telling her about us?" she asks.

"Only if you are." I was okay with telling the world, but even if Natalie is more comfortable doing it one person at a time, it's still progress.

She leans against the counter with a bemused expression, her arms crossed. "Look at us. Having friends and family over. Throwing a party."

We talked about doing that predivorce, but our world had closed in on itself until it was just us and Underwood Equity. I trap her against the counter, thinking of all the ways I can delight her beyond inviting her friends over.

"The first of many, babe." It was a promise. This is only the beginning, and there's no end in sight.

* * *

Natalie

Laughter drifts across the lawn. Kia tags Simon's legs and runs off. Maddy and Abby scatter, peals of giggles carrying across the yard. Simon sprints across the yard, his strong legs carrying him so far so fast that he's practically doing a slow-motion run to give the kids a chance.

As he runs, his shirt plasters to his broad chest. I've been watching him play more than I've been watching the kids.

"He certainly seems to be having fun," Mom comments. Normally, she'd be trotting around the yard, but she's not quite one hundred percent. My dad's wandering through the grass, making jovial comments about the game of tag and keeping an eye on Rachel's youngest, Braxton.

"He's always been good with kids." I take a sip of the lemonade Rachel brought.

She reclines in her chair, her head back and her sunglasses hiding that her eyes are probably closed. "All I know is that I owe you and Simon my sanity."

"That bad?" When I called, I half expected her to assume it was a pity invite and say no, but she offered up her special blueberry lemonade—which is really store-bought lemonade—and said she'd be here in a half hour.

"Not all the time. It's like they know it's a special day, but we were just staying home. Nothing was making Braxton happy and I felt like Kia was holding a contest for most ornery day ever."

Mom gets up and pats Rachel's shoulder. "When I'm feeling better, I'll offer up a day a month to hang out with them."

"You don't have to do that, Mrs. Wagner."

Mom brushes her off. "Janie or Nana. Hearing Mrs. Wagner makes me shudder. My mother-in-law was a hard woman. Anyway, an old retired lady can spare a day to entertain kids. Now, if you'll excuse me, I'm going to steal Abby's bed for a quick snooze, so I don't crash during the fireworks."

"Your family's amazing," Rachel says when Mom leaves.

"Yours would be too, if they lived closer."

She lifts her head and we both gaze at the revelry. Simon swoops down and picks up Braxton, tucking him into his arms without missing a beat of tag.

Rachel looks at me, her aviator sunglasses hiding her expression. "He's good with kids. Like, really good."

"He always has been. I think it's because he has the same energy they do. It's nice to see it channeled toward fun and not his job."

"Is it channeled toward you too?"

My cheeks warm. That's not exactly what she's asking, but Simon and I have expended plenty of energy on that topic. "He had a minor work emergency last night and he could be holed up in the office dealing with it, but he took care of what he could this morning and left the rest."

"That's improvement," she murmurs.

She was mildly surprised when I told her that Simon was

here and we were working things out. I haven't sensed a full stamp of approval, but she has so much on her mind while her husband's gone.

I can't hear what Simon's saying to the girls, but he's got them lined up and hopping on one foot with their finger on their nose.

Rachel chuckles when she sees what they're doing. "I guess Kia will be able to pass a DUI test when she's older." She lifts her chin toward them. "I had no idea that Abby looked so much like him."

"Maddy does too. She has my hair, so everyone thinks she looks like me." Something about what she says catches my attention. "Wait, haven't you ever met Simon?"

I met Rachel a few years ago, but we haven't been as close as we are now, not until we each had to be single parents. Have we really only crossed paths in kid activities or playdates? What about mom dates? Would our spouses get along?

"No. I feel like I know him from how much you talk about him though."

"I don't talk about him that much."

She rolls a droll look toward me. "If it's not the kids, it's him."

"Well, I mean..." She's right. There's not much else in my life but my family. Once I started training for my half-marathon, we talked about that and then my upcoming business venture. "I do talk about him all the time, don't I?"

"I'm sure I talk about Mike a lot."

Do I really talk about Simon ad nauseam? "Nothing noticeable."

"I didn't mean you go on and on. I just meant that once you came up with the idea to start Let Me Assist You and started training with Aleah, it was nice to hear you have something for yourself. Everything was wrapped up in Simon, and married or not, that's not healthy."

Oh. She has a point. I didn't have much going on for myself before my divorce that wasn't my husband or kids. I've been slacking on both my training and startup. I don't want to lose Simon, but I don't want to lose me either.

Simon trots over with Braxton propped on a shoulder. "One of us smells like he messed his drawers."

Rachel takes her sunglasses off and grins. "I'm going to guess it's my little man, but since I don't know you well…"

Simon laughs and hands him over. When she's inside, he plops in her chair, his arms hanging over the sides.

"Kia's got some speed on her, but damn, Maddy's a fast one. I think she kicked all our asses in tag."

"She's been racing in the yard since the snow melted. Claims she's practicing for soccer."

He blows out a breath and sifts through the cups on the patio table until he finds his. "If that's the level of kinder-gartners I'm going to coach, then I'm in trouble."

As if six little girls will even faze him. The real hurdle will be getting him to show up.

He takes a long pull on what's left of his lemonade, his throat working with each swallow. I'm just as helpless as I was in college. Getting distracted by his looks.

He finishes off his cup and turns his contemplative gaze toward me. "You don't think I'm going to make it work, do you?"

"I think you'll really try."

He watches me for a moment before he shoves a hand through his hair, ruffling it even more. Between that and his scruff, it's hard not to climb on his lap and just sit and enjoy the rest of the day touching him. That's what his casual look does. Makes him approachable. Touchable.

"You need to talk to me," he says quietly. "I didn't

know... until you told me it was already over. I didn't know."

I look around. Rachel's still inside and Dad's with the kids across the lawn. Mom's napping. This isn't a good time for a talk, but we have some privacy. "I did tell you."

"Not straightforward. Not 'Simon, if you don't listen to me, I'm going to divorce you.' All I remember are comments and I thought I was working on it. I thought I was doing as much as I could. I thought... I had time." He sits forward, the gravity in his gaze weighing his words down. "You were honest with me, but you weren't straightforward. If I fuck up again, you gotta tell me. Flat out, *tell me.*"

My nod is shaky. Honest, but not straightforward. I think of all the times I commented on his long hours, his absences, how he should've made the preschool graduation program since it was in the evening and not during the day when he was with clients.

Then I think of his responses. He can't pick his clients' time zones. It's the cost of growing. He can't waste the money Hayes left for him. Working from home is too disruptive.

And I left it. I kept leaving it as his final word until I left him.

"Okay," I say roughly. "I'll be straightforward."

His nod is the final boardroom deal one. We have the final terms of our arrangement.

Seventeen

Simon

Helena is across from my desk, her expression solemn as she updates me on the replies to the information we sent out yesterday. For the most part, we're in the clear. Our clients continue to trust us and Mr. Waterson is a prick. But we knew that.

She pushes a lock of hair behind her ear. I've never seen her less than put together, but she's downright haggard today. Her hair isn't in its normal twist, bun, or clip and there are circles under her eyes.

It's hard going to work the morning after the Fourth. Last night was probably a late one for her too. It gets dark well after ten p.m. this time of year, creating an early morning after enjoying a night of fireworks. She's probably just tired.

She checks her notes. "Tomorrow, I'll upload the job opening and start looking for larger spaces. How much personnel should I make sure it can accommodate?"

Right. My company is growing. It was a big deal to take on Helena and Charlie and a temporary mollification for my father, who thought I should have an entire building to myself with our last name fifteen feet tall and a fleet of financial advisers at my command.

He'll be delighted to hear I'm expanding. Getting real office staff instead of contracting minor duties. Only he'll disguise it as critiques and criticisms and couch it in comments about how this should've happened years ago—without my brother's money.

But I'm not expanding for him. I'm doing it for me. And partly for Helena, who looks thrashed and like a three-day weekend was half what she needed. I guess it was since she worked part of it.

"Let's start with a space that can accommodate four employees for now and we'll see what we find."

She bobs her head and checks her Apple Watch. "The first of your interviews will be here shortly."

Shit. I forgot those were today. "How many?"

"Three, but the news station is first, so be prepared for a camera."

Before I can dwell on how awkwardly crappy it'll be to field questions about my personal life, there's a commotion in the main area where Helena's office is.

"Girls, keep your voices down," Natalie hisses. "They could be on the phone."

Helena's expression lightens when the girls press their faces to the plexiglass windows flanking my door, their rainbow shirts and pink leggings instantly brightening the office. She waves them in without asking me first. "No worries. We're just reviewing the week ahead."

Natalie pulls the door open. The girls trample in, their arms full of containers. "Sorry. I just wanted to quickly drop off some leftover goodies from yesterday. I didn't mean to intrude." She flashes Helena a rueful smile. "I should've known better."

Maddy drops a plastic container on the floor. Celery and carrot sticks rattle inside. She picks it up and shakes it some more. "It's only the vegetables."

Helena laughs. "They can take a lot."

This Helena is one I've never seen before. Perhaps it was the tension between me and Natalie that subdued her so much before.

Natalie unloads a jug of lemonade into the fridge and sets a bin of Nana's cookies on the counter. She pushes her hair off her face and smiles sheepishly at me. I drink in the sight of her—sunglasses tucked into wild curls and bare legs. Not unlike the day we met while walking between campus buildings. I saw her and had to get to know her.

It was hard leaving a quiet house after such a fun day yesterday. Everyone was asleep while the sun streamed through the windows. I wanted to stay and make a fun breakfast, the kind with Mickey Mouse pancakes, sprinkles, and whipped cream, but I had to throw on a suit and grab some oatmeal instead.

"Thanks for the goodies. I'll need it to fuel me through all the interviews this afternoon."

Natalie grimaced. "Those are today?"

Helena gives her an apologetic smile, but I don't blame my assistant. If I had to, I'd do it again. We signed on a few new clients and inquiries come in every week.

Doesn't mean other parts of it aren't a pain in the ass.

Abby rounds the desk and pushes her way onto my lap. "What are you working on?"

"Abs, we have to go," Natalie says. "Dad's got a busy day."

I gently set Abby down and stand. "I do have to get to work, but you guys come by anytime."

The outer door opens and a young woman enters, holding the door for a guy with a camera. Dammit.

"I'm running while I can," Natalie whispers, giving me a wink, and herds the girls out of the office, nodding politely to the TV crew.

I hate to see them go, but if I can get through these interviews, I'll be done forever.

Helena greets the woman and shakes the man's hand before ushering them into the office. "This is Hailey and Carlton."

As the cameraman sets up, Hailey arranges the chair Helena vacated so she'll be out of view while peppering me with questions. "So, were those your kids?"

"Yes. Abby's the older one. Maddy's my youngest."

She sits and crosses a leg, a pleasant smile on her face. "That's so nice their nanny can bring them by when you're working. Makes the day shorter."

Awkward has already started. "Actually, that was my ex-wife." My throat constricts around the ex part.

Her brows pop. "Oh. That's nice. Are you two..." She shakes her head, her smile turning tentative. "Well, the article mentioned co-parenting, but are you two getting back together?"

I didn't think the local news would be bold enough to ask. North Dakota local news isn't known for hard-hitting investigative journalism. It often has as much fluff as facts. Doesn't mean we aren't nosy as hell and Hailey is probably genuinely curious, without the *should I ask this or not* filter.

How do I answer? Natalie wants to tell the girls. But I can't sit here in good conscience and brush my wife off like she isn't the most important part of my life. "We're working on being there together for our kids." Was that ambiguous enough?

Hailey scribbles down something on her notepad. "So,

what changes have you made in order to make that happen?"

I cock my head. Changes? Like, am I living at home but staying in a separate bedroom? That's all that's really changed to make it happen. "Excuse me?"

"Well, I guess that depends on why... um... what your definition of together is." This is as uncomfortable for her as it is for me, but she's sticking to her reporting guns and going for the heart of the story. "Adjusting from parenting together to co-parenting must've been rough. I'm sure you had to adapt. But if you're getting back together... I guess that'd depend on why you divorced. Things have to give if it's going to work out a second time."

Things have to give if it's going to work out a second time.

I'm sure you had to adapt.

It's hard to keep my mind on giving a congenial interview. I adapted to living in a sterile condo without my family. But did anything else really change?

Natalie remained at my beck and call.

And now?

I'm home more. That's something. It's a start.

And I told Natalie to be straightforward with me.

But... how much has really given?

The cameraman is ready and Hailey launches into her regular interview. I field questions about what I do, my role in the community, and my plans for the future. Part of me is still working over her earlier questions.

I'm expanding, and if I don't watch out, I'm going to circle back to square one and become eligible again.

* * *

Natalie

· · ·

What time is Simon's interview?

I send my mom a reply. **Tonight at 5.**

My parents will make sure they watch it. I doubt Simon's parents know a thing about his upcoming news appearance. Simon wouldn't tell them. I'm surprised he did that eligible bachelors article, but he likely didn't think about parental fallout. Since the article referenced him not being married to me anymore, they might've enjoyed it. Only Fargo news is not prestigious enough to register on their radar.

I put the phone down and flip a pancake. I've had a craving for them all day.

Abby leans over the counter to see the griddle. "Can you make Mickey Mouse?"

"That's Dad's thing." He has the patience, fitting the role of fun parent much better than me. I get bogged down in the minutia and he lives for the minute.

"What's my thing?"

I pop my head up at his voice. "You're home early. I didn't hear you come in."

He catches both girls in a hug and they rush off just as fast. He crooks a brow at their dismissal. "Mom gave them each a new pack of Lego Friends to play with this week."

"Right." His suit coat is nowhere to be seen and his tie is long gone. He unbuttons his cuffs and rolls his sleeves up. "I was just thinking about these today. Want me to do my special thing?"

"Yes, but we're out of whipped cream. Chocolate chips will have to do." I dig in the corner cupboard, saying over my shoulder, "I'm making supper early so we can watch your interview."

He pours a ring of batter, then two more at the top. His brows are drawn and I don't think it's from the concentration of making mouse-shaped pancakes. "We should talk to the girls first—about us."

I clutch the chocolate chips in my hands. "Is something wrong? Is it the interview?"

"No. I don't think so, but she was asking about you and us and I couldn't dismiss you completely." He aims a scowl my way. "She assumed you were a nanny."

I snort out a laugh. When Abby was first born, we couldn't afford a date night, much less a sitter. The irony is that now we could hire a nanny, but I want to either delay my career until my kids are grown or work it around their lives.

"Thank you for setting the record straight. So what'd you say?"

His jaw flexes. "I never really answered her question about whether we're back together, but I don't know what they're going to air or what angle she's going to take, and since how we deal with the girls is important to you, I cut out early."

He rushed home to save our secret from getting outed on the local news before the kids knew? If I hadn't fallen so hard for him already, that would've done it.

"I guess we'll be telling them while we're sticky with syrup."

"You don't mind?"

I set the chocolate chips by the spatula and risk burning the pancakes to slide my hand up his hard upper arm to his muscled shoulder until I cup his face. "Not when you came home early to make pancakes for them because you were worried about how it'd affect us."

The corner of his mouth tips up and he leans down for a quick kiss. It's the riskiest we've been with the girls awake since that first time in the laundry room.

Once dinner's ready, I call them down. They dive into

their chairs at the table and dig in right away, chattering about the Legos and the food. Simon looks to me to begin the conversation.

"Dad and I wanted to talk to you two about something."

"What?" Abby asks around a mouthful.

Simon jumps in. "Mom and I are... we'd like to... we want..." His pained expression makes me giggle. Maddy and Abby look between us.

"We're trying again." My explanation does nothing for them. They look just as confused as before. "We're kind of... back together."

Maddy's eyes brighten. "You're getting married again! Ooh, can I wear a big white dress and throw flowers?"

My mouth opens, but I have nothing to say. Another wedding is so far down on my list of possibilities that it's a nonexistent thought.

Abby pumps her fist. "I want to wear a dress too. Can we invite Kia and—"

"Abby." Simon chuckles nervously. "We haven't gotten as far as a wedding. We're just trying to make it work again. Your mom and I care for each other. A lot. We always have." His gaze is on me, its weight nearly tangible. "You've noticed that I'm staying here now. That's a start."

"You're moving into the guest room?" Abby asks.

My cheeks warm as I answer. "He's moving back into the bedroom with me."

Simon's steady gaze says so much but carefully reveals nothing to the kids about how often he's been in the bedroom with me already.

Maddy wrinkles her nose. "No wedding?"

I haven't thought that far ahead. Does that mean I think this is doomed? Or does it just mean that in my heart, I've always been married to this man?

Simon clears his throat. "Mom and I already had a wedding. But when we get to that point, we'll plan... something."

When we get to that point. He has no doubt. Do I?

I'm not sure and it's an answer I feel I should know. But it's barely been a month. We've only been divorced for almost eight months now, apart for ten, but it'll take more than a few weeks to repair what happened between us.

The girls go off about what they'd want a wedding to be like. Simon catches my eyes and shrugs. "That was easier than expected."

I smile. I don't know what I was expecting. The girls would think a conversation about which Disney princess is their favorite is more critical than me and Simon getting back together. Because, in their eyes, we already are.

I let out a quiet breath and cut one of my boring round pancakes.

"Are you okay with me moving back into the bedroom?" he asks low enough that the girls can't hear.

"Of course." I'm not. I want him in there, but it's a monumental step. My parents know, Rachel knows, and now the girls. Depending on how the news skews the interview, the Fargo viewing area might know too. I'm sure all our neighbors have come to the conclusion since his vehicle's been here almost every night for weeks.

And that doesn't bother me like I thought it would. But not having that barrier between us—different bedrooms—that's a big change.

Am I okay with it?

"What about the condo?"

Yeah. That. I ponder the subject a moment. I don't care about the condo as much as the bedroom. It was nothing but a separate bedroom for him, just across town.

"I'd like to sell it," he says.

He's so confident. But that's always been the dynamic between us. I'm the pessimist and he's the eternal optimist.

"I think that's a good idea."

His lopsided smile helps erase my doubts. I watch him lean over the table to help Maddy slice her pancake, not caring if he gets syrup on the front of his trousers. He came home early because of this. Because he cared what I thought.

If I truly have my husband back, then yes, I'm more than okay with having him next to me when I wake up.

He sits back down. "I think we should go fishing."

"What?" My question is drowned out by the girls squealing.

"I took Friday off. Told Helena to work from home. You said the girls don't have activities this week, so I thought maybe we could go camping."

"Where? With what?" We've never gone camping. I did with my parents when I was a kid. I don't see Phyllis and Trent Underwood as campers unless it's managing to rent a cabin in Aspen, just to say they did.

"One of my clients is loaning us his cabin by Detroit Lakes. It's small, but it'll be enough for us to get away and fish a little."

"Do you know how to fish?" I don't mean to be insulting, but... fishing? It's one of those things we talked about wanting to do regularly, but if we ever had time off together, we'd work on the yard or go to a park.

"Dad can fish," Abby proudly announces.

Simon grins. "You remember the stories of Uncle Hayes and me when we went to summer camp?"

Maddy furiously nods, her curls bouncing.

Summer camp. That makes sense. Not because they were sent for their own enjoyment and personal growth, but so their parents didn't have to parent.

"It's been a few years, but we can learn together," he assures them.

We watch his interview. Nothing scandalous is revealed. They concentrate on his work and what he offers to the community. The whole time he's on screen, the girls are delighted and I can't take my eyes off him, anticipation building after our talk at the table.

Not only did he come home early, but we're taking a short vacation. I don't know how relaxing it'll be, but I don't care. I'm looking forward to having my husband to myself, whether it's tonight in bed or out in the woods all weekend.

Eighteen

Natalie

"You even know how to build a campfire, Daddy?" Maddy's eyes brim with awe. The sun is setting and Simon's squatting by the firepit, turning on the propane.

"This isn't quite the same, but it'll still cook s'mores," he says as he clicks the button that'll fire it up.

His client's small cabin isn't what either of us expected. I thought it'd be rustic and when Simon said it was described as small, I expected all of us to share a room. We'd sleep on cots or maybe bunk beds with the girls.

But Simon's clients aren't broke and if they buy a cabin, it's a home away from home, a two-story place that's fancier than the two-bedroom house we rented right out of college. Rocks decorate the front face of the building, and it's made of logs, but it's decadent, with more than the comforts of home, like the hot tub on the back deck and the firepit with log furniture in the backyard.

We were even instructed not to worry about the kitchen

or bedding. The cleaning service comes every Monday in the summer.

If this is camping, then I'm on board. But I kind of liked the anticipation of roughing it, even if it was only a smaller cabin. We bought a backup tent just in case.

But if Simon's determined not to let work rule his life, then we'll have plenty of time to camp for real later. Maybe even later this summer. He wouldn't even have to take an extra day off for it.

When I look away from the flames, I find him watching me, his eyes hooded.

It's broad daylight and our kids are around, but that man can put my mind in a naughty place with one look. "It'd be fun to do more of this. Except, you know..." I gesture to the covered hot tub. "Without the amenities."

His intense gaze eases and he chuckles. "It's really nice here, isn't it?"

"I think the girls are going to get the wrong impression of camping." I turn to look over the lake that's at the edge of the yard. The owners even have their own dock with a beach that's shallow enough to swim in and deep enough to cast in. "And fishing."

Simon leaves the pit to stand next to me and drapes his arm around my waist. The girls frolic around the firepit. "My client apologized for not having the pontoon out here for us to use, but he said there's a canoe in the shed. I told him not to worry. It'll be all I can do to remember how to use a fishing pole again."

"After the girls see you start a fire, fish, and use a canoe, you're going to have to wear a superhero cape at home."

"S'mores over a propane fire doesn't count as a rugged survival skill."

It won't matter to the girls. And, watching him work the firepit and explain to the kids what he's doing, it doesn't matter to me either. This is Simon in his element. His real legacy. He thinks it's his work, but it's his family, it's living and experiencing life.

"I'll go get the hot dogs. Otherwise, they'll fill up on dessert."

He doesn't release me immediately and drops his voice low. "Now that we don't have separate bedrooms, do I get dessert tonight?"

"If we can wear them out so they go to sleep in their own bedroom instead of being too scared to sleep in a different house." I turn into him and brush my hand down his chest. "But... do you really want to meet your client next and think about how we banged in his bed?"

He winces. "Good point. That'd be more awkward than getting busted by parents."

I smile all the way to the house. Abstaining for the weekend isn't going to be easy, but it's not like this is a hotel. In the house, I gather all the supplies in the cabin while Simon and the girls lay out my dad's fishing gear on the porch.

We manage to make it through cooking the hot dogs over the fire without losing any inside the pit. The girls polish off a dog a piece. Next is s'mores. I gladly sit back and let Simon take the lead. I'd get too uptight with the girls around an open flame, but nothing about it seems to bother him. They follow his instructions and all three of them prepare a s'more for me first.

Simon's eyes twinkle as they hand them over on a plate. "Our way to show we appreciate you for making all this happen."

I accept the plate. The sincerity in his voice wraps around my heart. "It wasn't just me."

"I wouldn't have any of this if it wasn't for you." He squats next to me as the girls load up another skewer with a marshmallow. His fingers dance up my bare legs, causing a full-body shiver. "It's not just buying the groceries and packing, but all of it. We needed this."

We need this, but he needs it even more. There were more than a few times that I correlated how hard his brother worked and his death with Simon. It was terrifying. It still is. But we're here now.

"So we might be looking for our own lake cabin?"

He scans around the heavily treed property to the magnificent house, his fingers tracing up and down my leg. "I can definitely see the appeal, but I think we can downsize a little."

"Just a little?" This cabin and the property likely cost as much as our house.

"The firepit is nice."

"And the hot tub."

"We can get a hot tub." He flattens his hand on my leg and does the impossible—makes me forget about the melting chocolate on my plate. He used to be so preoccupied with the demands of his job that he didn't do this. But he's been touching me like it'll never be enough. "We can get a hot tub that I can actually do stuff to you in."

"You don't want to come in your client's hot tub?"

Simon exaggerates a shudder. "I'd never be able to look him in the eye again."

My laughter rings out and the girls give us curious glances before giving their attention back to their roasting marshmallows. My gaze caresses over his strong features and the humor shining in his eyes. He asked me to be honest about the negative stuff, but I have to be straightforward about the positive. He should know that too. "This last week, this last month, it's been so nice to have you around, for the girls to have their dad teach them stuff, like cooking over a fire and tomorrow you'll teach them how to fish.

Those are things they'll never forget and can pass down to their own kids."

His smile fades as he turns serious. "I've always wanted this for my family. I wanted to pass on my skills to the kids. To explore the world together. Stuff I never had with my parents growing up. Like, showing affection."

"I still worry that you'll try to do everything." I swallow hard before I say what I want to next. But he has to know my fear. "And I worry you'll end up like Hayes."

Surprise ripples over his face, followed by grief. He takes a moment to think about it and nods. He places his hand over my free one. "I know what's at stake now. I won't risk us again, Natalie."

"Dad," Abby calls. "Aren't you going to have one?"

"I'll be right there," he says over his shoulder. "Duty calls." His gaze skims the lake. "I should've asked your dad for a fishing review before we left town."

I laugh. "Dad's idea of fishing was letting the rod sit in the water while he visited with friends and I ate sunflower seeds and drank pop. We never caught anything."

"Then I'm one fish ahead of you." He moves back to the s'mores supplies and digs out his own Brody crackers and chocolate. The girls surround him and he lets them prepare his as he coaches them. They drink in everything he says. Simon can do no wrong in their eyes.

I used to be the same way, and I think I'm slowly getting back there.

* * *

Simon

.　.　.

"And then what does it say?" I ask Natalie as she holds the phone over my half-cleaned and gutted largemouth bass.

"I think the video will show you what to do better." She hits play and I watch, poised with a fillet knife over our supper.

"Eww." Maddy wrinkles her nose but doesn't look away from the person on screen cleaning a fish.

I mimic whatever they're doing because it's been fifteen years since I've cleaned a fish and even then, I was more of a spectator.

"Are we going to have something else to eat with this?" Abby's unimpressed with the whole cleaning experience, but I'm making them do it with me.

"We have plenty to eat." Natalie's voice is upbeat, but mostly, she's trying not to laugh at our spectacle. "And we'll each get a piece of fish if, you know, we get this part done okay."

I spear her with a scowl and she presses her lips together, fighting back laughter. Maddy's mouth hangs open as I cut away the skin. Abby loved the whole fishing experience, but I've lost her with this part.

"How are we going to cook it?" Abby asks. She lobbied hard for us to throw it back in, but I wanted to pass on a life lesson. Teach a person to fish and they'll never go hungry proverb kind of thing, but it's backfiring as I bumble my way through.

"Maybe we'll do some breading and fry it." Natalie readjusts the phone for me. "I don't trust our open-fire skills enough to keep from losing it in the flames."

"Can I cut?" Maddy asks.

"When you're older." Because we're totally doing this again. Not only because the more we do it, the better we'll all get, but because reeling the bass in was the most fun I've had in years.

As I follow the rest of the video's instructions, Natalie points out interesting parts of the guts—interesting to Maddy only. Abby's expression grows more horrified as she speaks.

"Okay." I set the fillets on a clean plate. "We'll cook some hamburgers too. Don't worry."

Relief crosses Abby's face and Natalie grins at me. She leads them inside with the meat while I clean up everything.

Four hours of fishing and we hooked one fish. Not bad for the commotion the girls were making on the dock.

By the time I get inside and wash up, the savory smells of our catch frying fill the kitchen. I dig out the hamburgers and go outside to cook on the grill my client keeps on the back deck. Abby comes outside. The look of abject disgust from earlier is still on her face.

"Don't like the smell of fish?" I ask.

She sprawls across the porch swing, one bony leg hanging down and the other across the seat. "So gross. Do I have to eat it?"

"No, but it'd be cool if you tried it."

"Maybe." She sounds like her mother when the girls ask if they can do something that'll make a giant mess and Natalie doesn't want to deal with the fallout of saying no right away. "Do we have to go home tomorrow? This place is really fun."

I'd love to stay another week. Hell, two. It's not like we're roughing it. I don't remember the last time I was this relaxed. Even when fishhooks were swinging left and right on the dock while the girls were learning how to cast their lines and I was certain I'd end up with an unintentional piercing, I was having a blast. My mind wasn't on work or checking my inbox.

"I'm sure my client has plans here the rest of the

summer, but maybe we can find another cabin to rent in August."

Her eyes light up. "Really? That'd be fun. Or we can use the tent."

My mind instantly forms an image of showing them how to put up a tent and build a real fire in a dirt pit. They're having so much fun this weekend. They'll really love going to another level of camping. "Yes. Let's make it happen. I'll talk to Mom."

"We should do it before soccer starts. You're coaching, right?"

Right. Coaching two teams. While I'm moving my office and training new staff. I can make it work. "I said I would."

She runs over and flings her arms around my waist. "It's so much better when you and Mom live together."

Just like me, the girls don't feel as if the divorce was real. It's a bad dream that keeps popping up with a reminder. Natalie's my wife in every way, except she's not.

I think about that all through dinner. Natalie lifts her brows in the middle of the meal. She senses something is off. I shake my head. It'll have to wait until the girls are asleep.

That time comes faster than any of us thought. Getting up early with the sun and then a full day outside, fishing and playing in the lake wore them out. Both Natalie and I tuck them in. One of the bedrooms has a queen bed they're sharing and we pile in and read stories. Natalie sneaks away first to take a shower.

After the girls fall asleep, I jump into the shower and clean all the lake water off. When I'm in fresh clothes that have no bug spray or sunscreen sprayed on them, I go looking for Natalie.

The house is quiet and I find her outside on the porch swing. She has a citronella candle burning and is peacefully staring at the water. The sun won't set for over an hour, but its rays ripple over the surface of the lake.

She hasn't heard me yet. I can look my fill without making her any more uncomfortable than a weekend of abstinence is causing. Long, toned legs rock with the swing. Her curls are drying into tighter corkscrews and despite the religious use of sunscreen, her cheeks and nose have a tint of red, making her freckles stand out.

My wife gets more beautiful each year. There's nothing more I want to do right now than carry her to bed, or hell, to the car so we can avoid all that uncomfortable "We fucked at your place" business, but I don't. We're not having sex, but we're still connecting. Natalie's always been my favorite person to talk to. My best friend.

I dig out my phone and bring up the camera. Focusing on her, I take her picture.

She senses me and blinks when she sees me taking her photo.

I pocket the phone. "You've been taking so many pictures, but there's not enough of you."

"Thank you." She smiles shyly and pats the spot next to her. We swing idly for a few quiet moments.

She inhales softly. The wind gently ruffles her curls. "I never understood why people kept a cabin and a house. I always thought it was twice the work. But this kind of relaxing is a different plane of existence."

"Abby wants to come here again next month."

Natalie looks at me. "What'd you say?"

"That it's a good idea. Maybe we can tent camp."

"I don't know if that'll be as relaxing," she says wryly. "But it sounds like fun." We fall silent for a few more minutes and watch pink and orange hues paint the sky as the sun begins to set. "What were you thinking about over dinner?"

"That I don't feel divorced."

"Oh." She goes still. My foot is the only one making the swing move, its faint squeaks fading into the night. "I guess that does raise some questions about what we do... how we're going to know that..." She blows out a gusty breath. "I don't want to plan a freaking wedding."

I chuckle and tug her closer to me on the seat. "I don't need a wedding to get married to you. But legally, we'll have to do something if we want to be officially married."

"The girls will want to be involved."

"Your parents?"

She nods, then quirks a brow. "Your parents?"

Both of us snicker. "I'll just go ahead and RSVP a no for them."

Natalie is my dream girl, but she isn't the one they pictured me with. They had visions of someone who came from money, already possessed a prominent name, and would demurely stand by my side while I ruled the world—all while they made comments about how I should've ruled the world a few years earlier if I was really that good.

I don't know if I was an accident for them, but I also wouldn't be surprised if it was *an heir and a spare* type deal. They just never thought they'd need the spare, and here I am, a family man living in the Midwest. How unimportant of me.

It was easier for them to blame Natalie for my perceived failures. At least they weren't the shittiest grandparents. When they were around, they loved hearing the girls' stories and my mother enjoyed chatting with them.

They just never come to visit and they travel so much that we can never plan to visit them.

Natalie lays her head on my shoulder. "How do we know?"

She doesn't need to clarify. How do we know when

we're solid enough to say our vows again? My answer is easy. "I could do it tomorrow."

She doesn't respond.

"Natalie?"

Lifting her head, she doesn't hide the indecision in her eyes. "It hasn't even been two months. I don't want to rush something so important."

I'm more crestfallen than I expected. Natalie's always been the more pragmatic one in our relationship, thinking of all the ways things can go wrong. Does she have to be that way when it comes to me?

I've just got to keep doing what I'm doing to earn her trust, to get us to a place where she has zero qualms about saying I do again.

We're just not there yet.

Nineteen

Natalie

Simon's unloading the car and I'm unpacking our bags and the kids are helping arrange the fishing gear so I can take it back to Dad. My mind's going a mile a minute.

The Fourth of July holiday stretched into a week with the trip and I haven't done anything to prepare for the kids' upcoming week. Groceries need replenishing, laundry needs to be done, and I haven't even looked at how behind I am on my own job and half-marathon training.

I zip into the office to peek at the calendar. Ugh. Swimming lessons start this week on top of their sports sampler activity.

"What's wrong?"

Simon's at the door, rugged and rumpled after a morning cleaning and packing.

I give him an appreciative smile. "It's nothing."

"That groan wasn't nothing."

I don't want to look at everything on my calendar I

won't be getting to this week. Nudging past him to leave the office, I head to the bedroom to gather a pile of laundry.

He follows. "Seriously. What's wrong?"

I look over his shoulder, but I don't see or hear the girls. "Where are the kids?"

His lopsided smile is adorable. "Downstairs, getting a TV fix after nearly *three days* without any."

As long as they're not around to hear, I can whine just a little. It's not like my issues are the end of the world. "I'm trying not to stress. It's a busy week and I need to run to the store and think of some lunches to pack so we can eat between their activities. Which is fine, but I haven't been keeping up on my training runs and I wanted to do a little more with my business before I launch."

My business. Compared to what he's built, my endeavor looks like a toddler game—for three and under. I'll get paid to do minor online tasks others don't want to. I'm not controlling millions of dollars, holding people's life savings in my hands, not to mention I won't have any employees.

He lifts a shoulder. "I'll go to the store. You go for a run."

"I should find their swimming things to wash first. Lessons are starting. And it's volleyball week. I think we have at least one set of knee pads."

"Go for a run. I'll do that."

"Don't you need to catch up?"

A cloud ripples over his features, then is gone. His neglected inbox and voice mails are killing him. "I'll do it after. I just need your help making a quick list."

He's been gone longer from work than I can remember. While we were away, he diligently ignored his phone to the point where he left it in the vehicle because it was buzzing with too many incoming messages and emails.

But he's willing to put it off a little longer because I'm stressed about first world problems.

I tilt my head. "Did I ever tell you how sexy it is when you get groceries?"

Heat seeps into his gaze and he shuts the bedroom door behind him. The click of the lock echoes between us. "Did I tell you how fucking painful it was not to mess around at the cabin?"

He reaches behind his head and yanks his shirt off. I do the same. He walks out of his shorts and underwear as he crosses to me, his erection pointing the way. I slip my clothing past my hips and wiggle out of them while unhooking my bra.

We don't mess around with foreplay. The kids could knock on the door any minute.

I put my hands on his shoulders and push him back on the bed.

His chuckle rumbles through my thighs as I crawl on top of him. He grips my hips to place me over him. All I have to do is rock down on his length.

His fingers tighten on my skin. "Any time you're stressed, I offer up my services."

I wrap my fist around his hot length to hold him steady and lower myself, releasing him when his broad tip breaches my body.

I don't bother to hold back my moan. "Definitely a good stress reliever." I don't care about anything right now. Not sports sampler camp. Not swimming lessons. And not running. All I'm focused on is getting off with my husband.

Our talk on the porch swing filters through my mind, but I push it away. It's tabled for now.

I press the rest of the way down and don't linger. Anchoring my knees on either side of him, I rock back up, then down.

"Natalie," he breathes as he rolls his torso up, stroking his hands behind me to bring us closer together. "Any time you need help, come to me."

I set a pace riding him and wrap my arms around his head, hugging his head to my chest. He makes me feel important, makes me feel seen.

"Simon." It comes out as a whine. Pressure's building. I need him. I need this. Just me and him against the world. That's what I've been missing. As an only kid who had a hard time making close friends, he's been my partner in so many ways. And when his work demanded more and more of him, I was left as that girl who had no one to face the world with. Only I had two little girls who looked to me for everything.

"I've got you," he whispers and slips his hand between us.

As soon as his finger touches my clit, I lose all thought. It's nothing but his strong embrace, him inside me, and a peak of pure bliss that's so close.

"I love you," I whimper. I might not be ready to put my heart on the line and say my vows again, but I can be honest. I love him. I've always loved him and that'll never change.

"I love you too," he says gruffly.

That's it for me. I explode, biting my lip to keep from hollering and bringing the kids to the door.

His hold tightens and he stiffens underneath me, rocking us both as he releases inside. He buries his head in the crook of my neck and rides out his orgasm as I finish mine.

Rolling us to the side, I remain in his embrace, but this time, it's my head in the crook of his neck.

His embrace tightens. "You don't know how scared I was that I'd never hear you say that again."

I sigh. "Same."

"I'm going to marry you again, Natalie. Whatever it takes."

I look up at him. "I hope so."

* * *

Simon

I take the girls with me to get groceries and put them to work hauling the bags inside and unloading them. Natalie was down in the gym when we got home, getting her run in.

The connection we had before I left...

That alone will make the next few hours of answering messages and emails worth it. But it was worth it long before that.

The girls are in their room, finding fresh beach towels for swimming lessons. I sit at the table and pull up my inbox.

Fuck.

Pages of messages. I set up an autoresponder like Lancaster suggested, but it seems to have doubled my emails. Mr. Waterson is demanding an update about the London startup that went under. He refuses to deal with Helena. Several more messages from Helena regarding all the work she was stuck with over the weekend.

I wince. She ended up working more than I thought because I was offline.

As I scroll through, I stop at the one from Brody Waite.

I hear you're expanding. My offer still stands.

I have no idea why he wants to buy Underwood Equity. Well, other than money. There are a lot of successful equity firms that are much larger and more established. Why mine?

I don't bother to reply. He's my brother's ex best friend. The fallout between them was more epic than I knew at the time, but Hayes's been gone for years. Is Brody looking out for me, or does he have it out for me?

I switch to voice mail and frown when I see my father's number. He didn't leave a message.

I flick my gaze to the stairs. The girls have been in their room for twenty minutes. Looking for beach towels has probably taken a detour into playing.

I call him back.

He answers with, "Simon. Where were you?"

"Sorry I missed your call. I took the girls camping this weekend." I refrain from saying *we* since I haven't told them that Natalie and I are back together.

"Ah." There's no interest in his tone. "Your mother and I have a flight to Singapore next weekend, but we thought we'd prolong a stop in Minneapolis and fly in and out of Fargo."

They never fly directly here. Coming to Fargo was an inconvenient diversion in their travel plans. When Hayes was alive, I'd hear about how much easier it was to visit him. How big his house was. How well his work was going. I don't get that anymore, but I know they're thinking it.

Are you sure that's the best route to take for investing? Shouldn't you have more employees by now? If you hired someone instead of working with Natalie, maybe you'd be better established.

"When are you coming in?" *Please be a weekend.* I'm so behind and I can't heap more onto Helena, but I also can't miss my parents.

"We'll fly in Saturday for lunch. We'll rent a car because the turnaround is pretty tight."

It doesn't have to be. They could come for the weekend. They could stay overnight. If they didn't want to stay here, they could get a damn hotel room. But Singapore calls.

They're never going to change, so there's no point in

bringing up any of those options. "Okay. We'll see you then. And, uh... Natalie and I are back together."

My father doesn't reply for a heartbeat. Then two. "Oh."

"Yeah. It's been almost two months." Not quite a month and a half. "And it's going well."

"Okay. Good. Yeah, good. Want me to tell your mother?"

"Sure. You can tell her the good news." I kept the wryness out of my voice. Neither one of them is going to think any of this is good.

"Yes. Of course. Saturday then. Looking forward to seeing the girls."

"They'll be excited to see—" He already hung up.

I set my phone down and scrub my hands down my face. Natalie's soft footsteps sound on the stairs.

"Did something bad happen while you were away?" she asks.

I peek at her from under my hand. Her wild hair is pulled back into a ponytail and perspiration glows on her skin. The flush on her face is deeper than after we finished our quickie in the bedroom. The concern in her eyes is for me. I have no idea why my parents don't see what a treasure she is.

I break the bad news, and I hate that my parents visiting is considered bad news. "My parents are coming next weekend."

She takes the chair next to me at the table. "Is it one of their turn and burns?"

"Yep. And I told them we're back together."

"Ah. Didn't go well?" After our college years, she's taken everything with my parents in stride, mostly because we haven't had to deal with them much. But it can't feel good.

"It's hard to tell. We'll have to see if they cancel."

"They need time to recruit one of their friend's single daughters to fly up here with them and lure you away."

Like the time in college, I went home to meet up with Hayes, but my mother had planned a dinner—with the daughter of her bank's president. Or the time when I wasn't allowed a plus-one for a family friend's wedding and was seated at a table with that same woman. It wasn't subtle, and it was horribly insulting to Natalie.

"They can bring an entire harem and it won't change anything."

She flashes me a smile. "I know. I need to grab a quick shower." She stands but pauses midway through pushing her chair in. "You know... I don't have to go. It could just be you and the girls."

Surprise lifts my brows. We've always made a show of solidarity. "You don't want to be with us?" At her flat look, I change my question. "You don't want to be my moral support?"

"Then who's my moral support?"

"I need you there," I say quietly. My parents' lack of visits doesn't make them any less stressful. The time between seeing them only compounds it.

She hides whatever she's feeling behind her resolve. "All right. I'll be there."

Relief beats at me. I know these meals are hard for her. She's practically ignored, but it's usually better than if my mother tries to talk to her. "Thank you. I owe you one."

"After Saturday, I may call it in."

Twenty

Natalie

I pick out my nicest slacks. Navy blue with a crisp seam. My cream silk blouse is next.

It's hot outside. And more humid than normal. Why am I wearing a silk blouse to meet Simon's parents?

Phyllis and Trent Underwood are not, and will never be, my biggest fans.

I need your moral support.

Buttoning up my shirt, I examine my hair in the mirror. Should I flat iron it?

My shoulders burn when I do it and then I'm left with a version of myself that I don't recognize and it makes me feel like the girl that's always trying to fit in.

I drop my hands from my collar and stare at myself.

Simon took that girl and gave her a place where she always fit in. When we divorced, I had to find it for myself. And I did. In seven months. Not bad.

But today is the highlight of sticking out. My differences

and any perceived deficiencies will be pointed out or alluded to. I can't care. What Phyllis and Trent think can't make a difference.

Simon enters the house. His voice rings across the place, calling the girls to load up.

He pops his head in the bedroom and stops. "Whoa. You look nice."

"It's going to be hot."

He shrugs. "The country club's restaurant will be freezing and Mother will comment that she needs a shawl."

My lips twitch. His perpetually cold mother does that every time. "And your dad will remind her that she left it in the car."

"I never figured out why she doesn't bring it in."

I do. It makes her stand out. Standing out in the Underwoods' world isn't a good thing.

Simon drives us to the country club. I swear he's only a member for the occasions his parents are in town.

Trent is opening the door of a dark sedan for his wife when we pull into the parking lot. Phyllis Underwood unfolds her long, glamorous body. Her pale-blond hair is in a tight chignon and she's wearing a purple sleeveless dress that fits every inch of her svelte frame and short black heels. No matter what her personality is, I'll always feel short and frumpy around her.

Trent closes the door after her. His smile widens when the girls race to him.

Phyllis feigns surprise and puts her hand to her chest. "Oh, my dears. Look how you've grown." She stoops to catch them in a giant hug.

They really do love their grandchildren. If they showed Simon half the warmth they show the girls, he might not be such a debilitating perfectionist when it comes to his professional life.

"Simon." Phyllis's voice holds sincere warmth I'm grateful to hear. She stretches her lean arms out wide and enfolds him in a quick hug, giving him a peck on the cheek. Simon ducks his head like he's embarrassed, but I know he treasures these rare affectionate moments.

As Simon exchanges an awkward back pat with his dad, Phyllis assesses me.

All warmth is gone and her familiar coolness sets in. "Natalie. Nice to see you again."

"Glad you could make it. How was the trip?"

"Well." She gestures around. "It was certainly a tiny plane."

Meaning there was no first class. "That's too bad."

Maddy tugs on Phyllis's dress, and usually, I'd try to curb her tendency to be handsy with loved ones, but I refrain. Phyllis clasps her hands together and delightedly listens to the story Maddy tells of her swimming lessons.

Trent even waits until she's done before saying, "Shall we?"

Simon escorts us inside and we're seated at a rectangular table. The girls fight to sit around their grandma. Phyllis is on one end, with Abby across from her and Maddy right beside her. Simon's on the other side of Maddy. I'm between Abby and Trent.

Simon starts in with business, making a few attempts to draw me into the conversation, but other than a polite smile and nod, Trent doesn't address my existence. Soon, they're talking nothing but business.

Turning my attention toward Phyllis, I'm relieved that she's deep in discussion about the *Frozen* movies and how she hasn't seen them and when the soonest she can see them is.

"How's Shayla?" Abby asks.

Phyllis's smile is bittersweet. "Doing well, I hear. She's also learning to swim."

"Do you get to watch her swim?" Maddy's practically sitting on Phyllis's lap, but my mother-in-law doesn't seem to mind. "Does she sleep over a lot?"

The smile turns sad. "No, she splits her time between her mom and her dad."

Abby tilts her head. "But I thought Uncle Hayes was her dad."

Phyllis's expression freezes and a line forms between her brows.

I squeeze her hand. "Remember when we talked about all the ways kids can have more than one dad or mom? It's like that."

"Aunt Kayla remarried?"

"Uh, no."

Phyllis's brows rise and she adopts the usual disapproving face she gets when she talks to me. An icy chill washes down my spine. What's she going to say? "No, dear, it'd be like if you weren't really your father's biological daughter, but he raised you without knowing that. Shayla has a biological father *and* one who raised her for her first few years."

Her pointed stare rests on me a moment too long. Does she think I cheated on Simon? That I lured him into marrying me?

Abby looks at me, eyes wide. "Do I have a biological father too?"

I barely keep from shooting Phyllis a glare. "Your biological dad and the dad who's raising you are the same."

"Unless your mom was to remarry." Phyllis's voice is sugary sweet. "Then you'd have a stepdad."

"But she won't." Maddy's voice overflows with confidence. "Mom and Daddy are back together."

Phyllis's smile is tight as she pats Maddy's hand. "So I hear. Tell me more about this summer camp."

Abby starts in on soccer and I smile fondly at every word, but it's fake.

Moral support. Simon's moved on to the stock market with Trent. Phyllis is taking advantage of the kids to ignore me. I'm stuck in the middle, twiddling my damn thumbs.

I shouldn't have come. I study the menu for way too long, rereading every entry at least ten times. When we finally order, I go for the cheapest meal option. Chicken something. I'll never give them a reason to think I'm a money-grabber.

As we wait for the food, everyone has someone to talk to except for me. Simon is justifying his business decisions to his father. Why can't Trent just talk to him like a colleague, at the very least? Phyllis is drawing pictures with the girls. My mom does the same thing, only she manages to chat with me at the same time.

Each minute ticks by excruciatingly slow until the food arrives. I'm grateful for something to do.

I take as long as I can to eat my food. Phyllis tells the girls how she had something similar to the pasta dish she ordered when she was in Paris. Only her description makes the Paris one sound like it was served on a gold platter and covered in diamond flakes.

The only item left on my plate is the mashed parsnips. I set my fork down and put my napkin on the table. "If you'll excuse me," I say to no one in particular and I don't know that anyone paid any attention.

My face burns as I make my way to the restroom. The chicken sits heavy in my stomach like a block of lead. A wave of nausea surges and then ebbs.

Slipping into the single restroom, I peek at the door next

to it. Good. More than one. I don't have to hurry. It's not like anyone will notice that I'm gone.

After I lock the door, I lean on the cool granite counter. My cheeks are flushed and my eyes are glassy. My stomach clenches and for a moment, I fear my meal is going to make a return trip.

I suck in deep breaths. I can't believe I'm this upset over Phyllis and Trent's treatment of me. The idea that I should be used to it doesn't make me feel better, but still. I should be used to it.

I close my eyes and take measured breaths. Eventually, the nausea passes and my energy is sapped.

I lean against the counter. God, I don't want to go back out there. I don't want to be in this silk blouse. I don't want to wear these pants or heels. I want to be in shorts and a tank top and yank some weeds out of my flower bed.

But I'm here. I'm being a good role model for the girls even if they might not understand it for years.

Does a good role model sit and sulk through the whole meal when one of the most important people in her life asks her to come for moral support?

He and I are together in this. I need to go out there and help deflect the hurtful comments.

I open the door. Simon's waiting against the opposite wall, his chin tipped down, his eyes searching mine.

"That bad?" His voice is low.

I peer down the hallway. His parents and the kids can't see us.

"I'm not feeling well." I let out a gusty sigh. "And yeah, it's the usual. Your mother gets in a few digs and then ignores me. Your father pretends I don't exist. But it's not going well for you, is it?"

His mouth tightens and he nods. "Think you can make it through the rest of the meal, or should we go?"

I wave my hand. "I'm a big girl. I can take it."

"You shouldn't have to."

"We're in this together. You have three number-one fans sitting at your table."

"They happen to be my three favorite people." He holds his arm out.

We walk back to the table with me tucked into his side. His father's back is to us, but his mother's gaze lands on us and jumps away, her lips thinning.

It doesn't get to me like it should've. I have moral support too.

* * *

Simon

"Do you talk to any of your old friends from Wharton?" Dad sips the last of his wine.

Looking at my dad hurts. I see an older Hayes. When we were younger, I never thought Hayes looked like Father as much as others claimed. But the last time I saw him, after years of working in the high-stress investment field and in a marriage that wasn't the fairy tale Hayes thought it'd be, he resembled our father. Fine lines fanning out around his eyes and a few grays popping out at the temples.

My father is almost all gray now. Mother probably would be too, but she'll never let anyone see it. Natalie once commented that they probably flew back to Pennsylvania every six weeks so Mother wouldn't miss a hair appointment with her trusted stylist. It's not a bad thing, but it says a lot about how Mother views life and how she wants everyone to view her.

But seeing her with her grandchildren is a revelation. Not once has she been anything less than supportive and loving. I don't know why her affections skipped a generation, but I won't complain. Natalie's parents are wonderful, but I won't take for granted that mine can contribute a little something to my family.

However, their treatment of Natalie is a problem. It didn't cause our divorce, but it's not helping us.

"Like Patrick? Or Karsten?" Dad's question yanks my attention back to him.

"Uh, no. Patrick lives in Hong Kong and Karsten retired early and moved to the Caymans. I heard he teaches diving."

Dad scoffs and takes another drink, his chest puffing. "Retired before thirty? More like he couldn't handle it."

Since Karsten started dabbling in drugs in college and then used them to fuel his long hours on Wall Street, I think rehab and retirement is the best decision he made. "He realized he didn't have to handle it."

"Well." Distaste turns Dad's lips down. "He's at the beck and call of his coworkers when they go on vacation in the Caymans and want to learn diving. Do you ever get a chance to row?"

"They call it kayaking here, Dad," I joke.

He smiles, but his disgust of living the regular man's life hasn't left. "Not one crew you can row with?"

"I've heard they're trying to bring the sport here, but I haven't had time to look into it." I don't miss rowing. Hayes rowed. Therefore, I was expected to row. His team won trophies. Mine didn't. All that practice for a sport I wasn't invested in means I don't care to touch a paddle again.

"You'd have more time if you hired a proper team to work for you."

"Like I said"—over and over—"I'm working on it."

"Well." That's my father's way of saying *I'd love to beat the dead horse of how I think you should run your business, which happens to be exactly like Hayes did, but I'll give you a pass and you should be thankful.* "Are you busy enough to expand though?"

"Dad's going to coach soccer," Abby interjects from the other side of Natalie. I didn't realize she was listening.

There's that fatherly frown of disapproval. "I guess you're not busy enough, eh, if you've got time to do stuff like that. Didn't you coach in high school?"

It's not an innocent question. It's more code, this time for *Don't teens coach because the adults have important jobs to do?*

"It's important to me to be a part of my kids' lives."

Father lets out a noncommittal grunt. They didn't even go to my parent-teacher conferences unless they were mandatory.

"Is it time, dear?" That's my mother's code for *I want to leave and you need to say it's time to go so I never look like the bad guy.*

Dad looks at his Rolex and winces, but I doubt he's remorseful. "Sorry we can't stay longer, but we need to get back to the airport."

Natalie packs the girls' stuff as they lead their grandmother out the door. I smile at the sight of my prim mother in her designer dress getting led out by each hand.

I drop my gaze to Natalie and my smile dies. Her mouth is set in a firm line and she's shoving crayons and notepads into her purse.

Father's not done with me yet. "Did I tell you that Crenshaw's daughter, remember the one you met when you were home sophomore year of college, moved back to Pennsylvania?" He chuckles. "She lives in the neighboring suburb. Small world. She runs a telecommunications company. The *head* of it. Pretty impressive for someone her age. I don't think she'll be quitting when she has kids or retiring at thirty."

My gaze darts back to Natalie. She stiffens but follows the same path to the exit as the girls and my mother.

"Good for her." Retiring at thirty doesn't sound bad to me. But there's no way I'll be in a position to kick back and quit. My company is at a critical growth level. I have several more years before I can take a back seat or even get away to the Caymans and take diving lessons from Karsten.

My father continues informing me about Crenshaw's daughter and her job as we walk out. Natalie's standing by the passenger door of my car with her arms wrapped around herself. The girls are playing around in the back seat of my parents' rental.

"Go get loaded up," I order the girls. Nerves tighten in my gut. Is Natalie feeling like crap because of my parents? And I'm the one that asked her to come when she didn't want to.

I meant it when I said I'm not messing up my second chance with my wife. And that means something needs to be done.

I didn't wake up today thinking I'd need to confront my parents. I've never done that. Not about the way they treated me versus Hayes. Not about the way they treat Natalie. And not about how little they're truly involved in my kids' lives.

That ends today.

After the girls give my parents another round of hugs and run off, I steel myself. "Listen." Something in my tone makes them pause. Neither one has gotten in the car yet. "I've never said anything before, but I'm rectifying that. You need to treat my wife better. She's the love of my life, the mother of my kids, and I don't want to lose her. If that means cutting toxic people out of my life, then..."

"What the hell are you saying?" Father blusters. "We've never said anything bad to her."

"Simon…" Disappointment oozes from Mother.

I shake my head. "I know I'm not Hayes and that I'll never live up to him. I know you'd rather he was around and not me, but I can't control that. I love Natalie. She's shown me how to really care for someone and I don't want to lose her. So, I'm serious. If you can't treat her with respect and cut out all the subtle digs and the cold shoulder, then I'm sorry, but I can't expose the girls to seeing their mother get treated that way. I love you both, but that's where we stand."

I give them a sharp nod and walk away before an argument starts. Natalie and the girls are loaded up, but her questioning gaze is on me. My expression must tell her it wasn't a congenial goodbye.

When I slide into the driver's seat, all I say is, "Tell you when we get home."

The drive is quiet and the girls run inside as soon as I park. I stare out the windshield, my chest tight, as I tell Natalie what I said.

She twists her hands. "I can't believe—"

"That's the problem." I twist in the seat so I can face her properly. "You can't believe I'd stand up to my parents for you. I should've done it years ago. I'm sorry."

She rests her hand on my pecs as if she senses the turmoil inside. "I feel guilty as hell. I can't imagine how hard it was for you. Have you ever…"

She knows the answer. I've never told them what I really think.

"I wish it was more of a release, but it was… disheartening. Because I don't know if I'll ever see them again." I don't know if they'll ever get over themselves enough to try to be in our lives.

But it was necessary, and I'll do whatever is necessary to save this marriage.

Twenty-One

Natalie

I puff through the plank that Aleah is running me through. She counts down, but each second feels like a minute.

"Good job," she says as she resets her timer.

I drop to the floor and lay my head on my arms. My gut is aching from my third set of planks, but it's nothing unusual for working with Aleah. Not to mention that I haven't been diligent about my training the last month or so.

I've been tired. Just worn out down to my bones.

I hope I'm not sick, but I haven't been able to shake this icky feeling since the day Simon cut his parents off. That was three weeks ago. My half-marathon is in two weeks and I don't think I've got even a four-mile run in me. The long runs I've had to do turned into a jog-walk ordeal.

"You're flagging today, my dear." Aleah sits with her legs crossed on the mat next to me. I hope that means I get a rest.

"I'm tired." I roll to my side and prop my head in my hand.

"Not sleeping well?"

"I don't think it's that. I've been feeling run down for a while. Probably because I haven't been training enough."

She narrows her dark eyes. "Do you think you've been overtraining?"

Do I look as guilty as I feel? "Definitely not. I've missed a few workouts"—I grimace— "each week."

She smiles, but she's still considering me. "How's Mr. North Dakota?"

My face heats. We've been great. Tighter than ever, especially since the fallout with his parents. "He's still busy but making more of an effort. His assistant has started sifting through applicants, and they might move buildings soon, but we're good."

"And your work?"

"It's just waiting for my go-live date. Everything's done really. Once I launch, I might be a little busier, but not until I sign a couple of clients. That won't be until after school starts anyway."

She takes her eyes off me and scans the gym. It's only midmorning and the place isn't very busy. My mom took the girls so I wouldn't be so terribly behind on training when I toed the starting line. If I didn't come today, I knew I wouldn't do anything, much less my training run. I didn't do my long run this week. Or last.

She glances at the trainer working with her client by the mirrors. They're the closest ones to us, then she quietly asks me, "Do you think you could be pregnant?"

I sputter and laugh, but my smile freezes. Could I be?

Aleah lifts a shoulder. "I remember when you told me what a surprise Abby was since you were on the pill. It's none of my business though."

"No. I mean, I don't think..." Oh God. Nausea. Tired all the time. I don't care who can see, but I palm a boob. Yeah, they've been a little more tender lately. "Shit."

"Sore?"

I nod, my vacant stare stuck on the hot-pink mat Aleah's sitting on. "How could I let this happen?" We didn't use a backup before because it never mattered if I got pregnant. Our plans for more kids got pushed to the side as *well if it happens...* What if it happened?

While we're divorced?

"No need to get worked up until you know for sure." Aleah's calm voice breaks into my thoughts. "But I think since you're so worn out, we can cut the run a little short."

"If I am pregnant, what do I do about the race?"

She lifts a shoulder and she'll never know how much I need her unflappable personality right now. "It's up to you and how you feel. Most moms are just fine. You were training before and we aren't changing it much before you'd need to do it. Stay hydrated. Rest. But I'll give you the official response and tell you to talk to your doctor." She leans forward and gives me a wink. "Just make sure it's a doctor that knows what they're talking about."

I roll back to my stomach and drop my head into my hands. "Oh my God, Aleah. I wouldn't even know how far along I am."

She chuckles. "You wouldn't be the first one. Babies don't always look at the calendar. But I'm going to repeat that you don't know yet."

I lift my head. "I need to find out."

Her expression is rueful as she stands. "I had a feeling you'd say that."

I force myself to take the time to clean up, but it's the fastest shower ever. After getting dressed and throwing my hair in a ponytail, I breeze out of the gym.

Do I buy the pregnancy test and take it before I pick the kids up? Mom's used to me running an errand or two after my appointments.

No, I'm going to buy it and take it in the store. I have no plan of what store I'm going to go to, but I drive in the direction of my parents' place. I pass a grocery store with a pharmacy and swing in.

Finding the pregnancy test is no problem. It's like there's a homing beacon. My gaze darts around, looking for familiar faces. This act always feels so private. My life is in a major transition right now and I'd rather not share the news —if there is any news—with anyone else.

I find an open self-service checkout and I whip through, stuffing the test in my purse after paying. My luck is riding at one hundred percent. There are bathrooms by the entry and exit doors.

I scurry into the women's restroom, crouching in on myself as if it's going to help make me invisible. It's empty, so I duck into a stall and rip the packaging open.

Going through the all-too-familiar process takes me back to finding out I was expecting Abby. I did the same exact thing. I didn't want to risk bringing the test back to my dorm room, so I ducked into a department store bathroom and hid all the evidence when I was done.

Okay. I go through the pee-on-a-stick procedure. I only have to wait a minute, and I count each second.

I can't tear my gaze off the mustard-yellow door of the stall. If I thought Aleah's minute plank ticked by slowly, this sixty seconds is eternity.

My heart's slamming against my ribs when I look down. Positive.

* * *

Simon

The house is quiet as I ease through the door. It's almost nine. The last few nights, I've come home late, but this is the latest. It's still earlier than before we divorced.

I toe off my shoes and refrain from calling out for anyone. Since it's summer and the girls go to bed later than a school night, I go to their room first.

Only the light between their bedroom and the guest room is on. Murmuring and giggles drift out of the room.

I lean in the doorway. "Are my girls awake?"

"Daddy!" Maddy rolls off the bottom bunk and runs for me. Abby clambers over Natalie. I give them both hugs as a subdued Natalie crawls off the bed, her smile wan and half-hidden by shadows.

As I finish tucking the kids in, Natalie ghosts out. My husband intuition is strong. There's something wrong.

I expect to find her on the couch, in the kitchen, or even doing laundry. But she's in our bedroom, sitting on her side of the bed, her hands gripping the edge. I close the door and drop down next to her.

"Need to talk?" I ask.

"We have to." We sit for several moments before she speaks again. "I'm pregnant."

My world comes to a standstill. She's... we're... "Holy shit."

"Yeah," she says with a rasp.

A baby. A bigger family. Just like when I felt like I lost mine, we're expanding in the tiniest but most momentous of ways. Another kid.

I can't stop my smile. Throwing my arms around her, I hold her and laugh.

Her own laughter starts, stilted and thready, but gains in confidence. "I knew you'd be thrilled."

There's enough gravity in her tone to warn me. I let her go enough to look at her, to see her expression. She sucks her lower lip between her teeth, her eyes brimming with anxiety.

"You're not as excited." Part of my elation plummets. I know this is unplanned and kind of an unusual time, but we both wanted more kids.

"Yes, I am. Sort of." She pushes her hair off her forehead, holding it back as she stares at the carpet as if she sees patterns where there's only solid print. "Not only are we divorced, but I had plans. I'll always welcome a baby. I love kids. I love our kids. But I was just..."

"Just what?"

She switches her focus to her fingers, twining against each other. "Reclaiming myself. For so many years, I've been a mom. Wife. Simon Underwood's assistant. Dreaded daughter-in-law." We share a small smile. "But the last few months, I've been able to figure out what interests me. As an adult. We were just kids when we met, then I was a mom, and we had the company, and I had no hobbies of my own that didn't involve scheduling your appointments or reloading a diaper bag."

Because I wasn't around. I was gone so much that she couldn't be Natalie Underwood. I separate her hands with mine, keeping them all wrapped together. "I'm around now."

"Yeah. You are. I want to be excited, but my mind is stuck on *now what*?"

"How far along?"

Her low chuckle has only a hint of humor. "The first time I felt sick was when your parents were here, but I have no idea."

"Nice."

She giggles and elbows me. "It's so very junior year of college."

"One day, we're going to figure out what's causing it."

"You've said that every time now."

"Still funny." I draw her into my arms and fall back. Our legs are hanging off the bed and I'm still in my slacks and button-down, but my tie is long gone. I'm like Superman leaving the office. Stripping out of my clothing as soon as I can. I miss my dad uniform of shorts and a T-shirt.

I miss my kids during the day.

Today, I even took a quick break, which I never do, and searched online for soccer drills for five- and eight-year-olds. Lately, I've been catching myself drifting off, thinking about other fun family things I can do with the kids. Or activities we can do while Natalie does her own thing.

Now we're going to have a baby again. I think back to Abby and Maddy as babies. I did the midnight diaper changes and all hours of the night feedings. I was here if they were sick—at night. I missed their first rollover. Natalie was the one who discovered tiny little teeth pushing through. First steps? Missed those.

It didn't matter if those momentous events happened on the weekends. I was gone.

"I'm going to be there," I say again, unsure if it's for her benefit or mine.

"I know you want to be."

Ouch. "There are going to be days…" She knows all that. She doesn't want to hear me promise it. She wants me to keep that promise. "Don't worry. It's early yet, the beginning of August. You can't be more than what, six weeks along at the most?"

She nods, her soft hair tickling my chin. "Probably. I'm sure I forgot a pill or two when the girls were sick and then just never noticed that time of the month was so late."

"When do we tell the girls?"

"I'd rather wait for the second trimester."

Which might be sooner than we know. "Your parents?"

"Same."

"What about your work?"

She rolls on her side. "I've been thinking about that. I don't want to walk away entirely, but I thought that maybe I could still launch but only accept a light client load. And it might be slim pickings when I tell them I'll be off for maternity leave, but some people might just be looking for someone to jump-start their social media or calendar planning. Get them into a routine they can keep up with. They might not want long term."

Energy infuses her when she talks about Let Me Assist You. She's excited, and she's been waiting. I need to make sure she'll get the time she needs.

I roll to my side to face her. Being this close and on our bed is enough to wake my dick up. Talking about our future together sends more blood in that direction. I tug her closer. She tilts her chin up, and I want to do what I'm good at—showing her how much I love her by loving her body.

But the need to comfort her hasn't left. "It'll be all right."

"I know." She starts unbuttoning my shirt. I lean back to give her more room, grateful that she's up for sex. "Is this the part where we have sex right away after I tell you I'm pregnant?"

That's how we handled the news in the past. "I'd hate to ruin a perfect record."

Her breath wafts over my chest as she laughs. She's made it down to my pants and works on the button and zipper. "I've been remembering those other two times all day and I have to admit that I need this now."

She frees my erection and wraps her fingers around it, stroking up and down.

I groan and roll as flat on my back as I can. Since I leave for work first, the bed's not made and a wad of blankets is under my shoulder. I'm not going to let it deter me or her.

She gives me a few more pumps before wiggling out of her bottoms. I'd like to do more to her. I'd like to throw her legs over my shoulder and make it impossible for her to hold in her cries. I'd like to shut the lights off in the house and take her to bed for the night, using as much time as I need.

But I sense her need for control in a situation she has surprisingly little control of. She loves her kids, but she wants more. It's her daily schedule that's going to have to change and morph to fit the new addition to our lives.

None of the rest of our clothes are removed and I think she's going to straddle me when she says, "I want to feel your weight on me."

Control and security. I can give her both.

She lies back and I sit up and do as she asked, but I don't push inside of her. My cock is pinned between us, her blistering-hot center only inches from it, but I ask, "Now what do you want me to do?"

"I want you to..." She sucks her lip back between her teeth and her face flames. "I want you to fuck me."

It'll always be sexy to hear my wife say that. "Slow? Fast?"

"Fast. And... hard."

I readjust, wetting myself in her slick heat and thrusting inside. Fast and hard, I pump, and she clings to me. I can't get to her breasts through her shirt, so I dominate her mouth. Our tongues clash and our teeth bump together as the force of my hips and hers shake the bed.

I should be able to last longer, but thanks to the way she's writhing under me, wanting more, wanting it harder,

I'm ready to blow. I manage to hang on until her legs clamp around my hips and her walls convulse around me. Her cries mingle with mine, but we stay locked at our mouths and our hips as we ride our crests. Heat blooms between us and I barely notice my pants stuck around my knees or my shirt bunched around my shoulders.

I release the kiss but keep my forehead touching hers.

"I needed that," she says.

"I'll always be there for you—especially when it comes to sex." I gently leave her body and help her stand. "I'll shut the lights off and come back to bed."

She ducks into the bathroom and I toss my shirt into the dirty laundry. I remove my phone and kick out of my pants. There's an email notification from Helena.

I peek at the bathroom. It won't hurt to check the email. I don't have to act on it.

I *won't* act on it. Natalie needs me tonight. She'll feel better if she can go to sleep with me, not being balls deep in my phone.

But I bring it up just so I know what to expect in the morning. I don't make it past the first sentence.

This is my notice of resignation.

Twenty-Two

Simon

Things had been going so well. I drum my fingers on my knee, waiting for Helena to talk. We have an hour buffer before I start meeting with clients and I want answers.

Why now? Why not after we moved and trained new staff? Why *fucking* now?

I'm supposed to coach soccer, for God's sake. *Two* teams.

Helena looks like shit. Her hair hangs limp on her shoulders and her back is stooped like she's carrying the weight of the world. I have a fleeting hope that her resignation was an impulsive send and that she had a good night's think on it and sees that this is the best job ever and wants to stay.

Is it the best job ever? Would I recommend working for me?

That thought stops my drum solo at the same time as she answers. "It's the hours. I might not always be in the office, but I've been working seventy to eighty-hour weeks.

Even before the beginning of June, it was sixty hours a week."

My forehead crinkles. "Is it the pay?" I'll double it. Fuck. I'll triple it. She's a good employee, and she's also helping me save my damn marriage.

"It's not the pay, it's my son."

"You have a kid?" Why wouldn't she tell me she was a mom? As a boss, I can't ask. She doesn't even talk about her husband.

There's a brief smile as she says, "He's four."

"Oh. Why didn't you say anything?"

"You're a work-driven boss, and my previous boss was less than considerate when I needed to take a sick day and that was after how affronted he acted about maternity leave."

"Family comes first, Helena. You never had to worry about that."

Her glacial blue eyes are dubious. "I missed my vacation in June because you had to be around for your wife." She holds her hand in a no-offense pose. "Which is great. But it's been like that for the last two months. We canceled our family vacation, I missed the Fourth of July, and really, I haven't been around much since I started working here. My husband's been great, but I want to quit before my own marriage is wrecked."

Her eyes go wide and her back hits her chair. I feel better that she can't believe she said that, but it also makes her statement sincere. She's afraid of the toll this job is taking on her personal life.

She was supposed to go on vacation? *Shit*. I vaguely recall her asking for approval. "Helena—"

"I'm sorry, Mr. Underwood, but I need to step back and think about what else I can do with my career. We want to have more kids. I want flexible work, and Underwood

Equity can't provide that. I can't dedicate the next six months to a year training an assistant, and then we have another period of growth and I'm back at square one. Not to mention that your personal assistant is done with his degree soon and will be moving on."

"Charlie's going to school?" Why is this the first I've heard? Are my employees afraid of me?

"He's finishing his MBA in December." She peers at me. "Didn't you know?"

"He hasn't mentioned anything." Charlie and I barely cross paths. Our interaction is mostly through messages.

"I thought I should resign in time for you to replace me before he leaves."

"No, I understand. I'm sad to see you go. You're good at what you do." I just wish she would've talked to me.

And then what would've changed? I would've worked more and my homelife would've suffered.

The weight of her decision lifts from her shoulders and she's back to confident professional. "Do you want me to comb through the applicants and see if there's one who'd be a good fit for this position?"

That means I have to train them. Looks like moving my office is put on hold. "No, I'll wait on that, but you can start writing up a job description for your position."

We transition to normal beginning-of-the-day business talk and I try to concentrate on more than wondering what the fuck I'm going to do.

I manage to be mentally present for all my clients, but the day stretches longer than I want. I send Helena home after a normal workday. Her last two weeks with me don't need to be miserable.

They might be bad for me.

The later I work, the clearer it is I need an executive assistant and I need one fast.

I know of one.

No, she wouldn't go for it. We've been there before.

But we've been there and it really worked—for years.

I close down everything and shuffle my papers into a pile, then lock up the office. I breeze home, thinking about how I'll approach Natalie with my suggestion. It's got to be a plan that works for us both. After last night, it's my priority.

I rush home and get there in time for bedtime. The girls give me hugs and then rush upstairs for story time.

Natalie lingers behind. "How'd it go?"

I lift a shoulder. "As well as it could've. I'll be there for story time and we can talk after that."

The girls con us both into reading a book they've each picked out for us. Four books later, Natalie and I emerge from their bedroom.

She floats down the stairs and goes right for the dishwasher. There's a full load inside and a pile of dishes by the sink. I jump in to help unload.

"What did Helena say?" She sounds tired. With both Abby and Maddy, her first trimesters were ridden with fatigue and stomach issues. This one seems to be no different.

"She's burned out. Everything you warned me about."

She nods, but doesn't throw around an I told you so. "I hope she finds a good fit. Did she give longer than a two-week notice?"

"No." After seeing how determined she was to be done, I think I'm lucky to get that much time. I take a deep breath. Time to go for it. "So, we were going to hire an assistant for her, but now that she's done, it's a higher priority to get a new executive assistant."

"Makes sense." She stacks plates and I get the cups and glasses.

I go for the hook, hoping like hell she'll be receptive. Because if she's not, I have no idea what I'll do. There's only one me and I'd need to clone myself a few times to do everything I want to.

"So, I was thinking that since you're starting a business similar to what I'm looking for, I can hire you."

She stills, a pile of plates in her hands. "As an assistant? But you need to hire one full time anyway."

She's cautious, but it's not a no. I can work with not a no. "Right. I can do that, but if you work as my executive assistant for a while, it will give me time to hire one properly."

The plates get set down. She presses her fingers to her forehead. "I'd be your executive assistant?"

"Yes." I tighten my grip around the girls' red plastic Lego cups. *Please. This would solve so many issues for me.*

She levels me with a steady gaze. "No."

* * *

Natalie

"No?" Confusion clogs Simon's dark gaze. He really thought I'd do it.

Anger mounts, with old resentments trailing not far behind. Did he think I'd jump up and down, clap my hands together, and rejoice that I got my first client? No. Just *no.* "I know how this ends."

"I only need a little help. It'd be temporary."

I plant my hands on my hips, trying not to take out the brunt of my irritation on him. My hormones are on a roller-coaster ride. I'm tired, and just when I thought we turned a corner, the path is leading us back to the beginning. And he doesn't see it.

"We've done temporary," I say. "It lasted for years."

He cocks his head like he didn't hear me correctly. "I've made a concentrated effort to change. We won't make the same mistakes."

"Meanwhile, what? I turn down other clients because Underwood Equity is dominating my time? And I'm basically your employee again? Then the baby's born and I'm back to answering your messages while I'm rocking a newborn? Working all through naptime because you don't set boundaries for your clients?"

"That's not fair, Natalie. That's the past."

"That's the present," I snap. Just because he learned to set autoresponders doesn't mean he wasn't up half the night answering messages when we came back from the lake. Who knows how much of that weekend Helena sacrificed? "That's exactly why Helena quit."

"I get it," he says from between clenched teeth. "I've been telling you for two months that I get it. I've been proving it. Natalie. A few months is all I'm asking."

"No, you're asking me to use what I'm building for me for *you*, to turn my identity back to revolving around you."

He thumps down the plastic cups and I flinch. "That's not what I'm asking. I gave up my *parents* for you."

My jaw drops. Did he go there? "I didn't ask you to." My index finger has a mind of its own as I wave it around. "But let's talk about that. I put up with their shit for ten years. Ten years of being belittled, dismissed, and standing by while your mother tries to set you up with someone else. And you finally have a two-minute talk with them and think it's all better?"

He pinches the bridge of his nose. "Look... I'm sorry. I'm sorry about them, I'm sorry about working too much.

But I've built this from the ground up. I worked that hard for us, for the girls."

And there it is. The excuse he falls back on. When he says it, he thinks the argument's done. All is explained. "You don't do this for us."

His jaw clenches. "How can you say that? Of course I do. There's no other reason."

I've been quiet about this too long. He asked for straightforward, then he's going to get it. It's not just his work hours that affected our marriage—it's the real motivation behind it. "You have something to prove, and it's not to me and it's not to your kids. You're so stuck on not living up to your brother's reputation and trying to do something that'll make your parents say 'attaboy' that you couldn't see what it's doing to you. Or your family. And you're doing it again. Do you know how many times I wished Hayes never left us that money?"

He braces one arm on the counter, the other on his hip, and gives me a hard look. "Don't bring Hayes into this."

"He's been in it from the beginning. You were so driven in college because when you accomplished something, your parents pointed out how Hayes accomplished more. When he passed away, that money was supposed to be his last gift to you, but it's like a curse. You want the glory for yourself. That's why you didn't expand and hire someone when I first started telling you that it's too much. It was too much for me, it was too much for you, and it was too much for us. Now you want to go back to that?"

We lock gazes for a few long moments. If the girls can hear us, they haven't come looking yet. They've never witnessed us arguing like this.

He works his jaw before he asks, "Are you asking me to choose between work and you?"

"No, Simon." Defeat rings in my voice. "I'm not asking

you to choose. I'm saying that I'm tired, and I don't know if I'm willing to do the last few years all over again." I inhale a long breath and stroke my gaze over his strong jaw and his perfectly combed hair. I miss tousled Simon.

His voice gets thick. "Then what are you saying?"

I roll my lips in and close my eyes. Last night, we connected on a deeper level than ever before. And yet here we are. "I don't know what I'm saying. I have a lot to think about."

I leave the dishes and go to the bedroom. It's early, but I don't care to rehash the same exhausting discussion with my ex-husband.

But escaping to the bedroom backfires. I see us on the bed, naked and entwined. I see him holding me. I see my hopes for our future crash back into reality.

I cross to the dresser and grab my night shorts and cami. I'm too exhausted to cry. Too afraid to look back on what I said to Simon in the kitchen and wonder if I went too far. Too afraid to think that Simon is going to make a choice and it won't include me.

Twenty-Three

Simon

I glower out the window of the plane. Helena spent the morning calling and messaging all of my appointments for the day. Canceling them.

When I land, I'll start on tomorrow's schedule.

My yawn can't be stifled. I got almost no sleep. After putting away the dishes, I gave Natalie time, deliberating whether I was allowed in the bedroom to sleep or if I should retire to the guest room.

I didn't want to sleep in the fucking guest room, so I went to sleep in my own bed, but sleep is a strong word for what happened. While Natalie tossed and turned next to me, I stared at the ceiling, replaying everything that happened before I went to bed and moving back in time.

The night before, when she needed me to comfort her. The baby news. Further back to our fishing trip. The Fourth of July. Our time apart during the divorce. My sterile, boring condo. Sleeping alone. Last year, to a pale, withdrawn but determined Natalie and her lawyer filing the papers I signed.

I let my mind wander the time line of my life all the way back to the day I met Natalie. When I laid eyes on her, my world exploded in Technicolor. The first time I made her smile and laugh, I was a man addicted to everything she offered.

Is it still like that?

The trip down memory lane was enlightening and I rolled out of bed and left before Natalie woke.

I rub my eyes. The only open seat was in first class, which I don't mind. More space to poach myself in my thoughts and feelings. Because after I reviewed my life with Natalie and the kids, my brain focused on Hayes.

We weren't as close as I wanted to be. As a kid, he was always involved in an activity and since he was older, I could do nothing but spectate. Then he went off to college and he was closer to Brody Waite than he'd ever be with me. After that, it was marriage and his work in holdings—with his wife.

Am I trying to mimic his life? Am I working only to prove I'm as good as he is?

Because if that's the case, then when my brother left me all that money, I attached a metric ton of expectation to it.

You were so driven in college because when you accomplished something, your parents pointed out how Hayes accomplished more. When he passed away, that money was supposed to be his last gift to you, but it's like a curse.

A curse. I saw it as nothing but an answered prayer, but that money destroyed my family. I received it and I doubled down. Tripled down. I grew Underwood Equity past my capabilities.

Because that's what Hayes did.

And he died of a heart attack.

If I'm determined to follow in his footsteps... well, I've seen the finish line.

I swallow hard and look out the window. Skyscrapers tower over shorter buildings. Cars bustle through the streets.

It took a while for my last conversation in Chicago to make sense, but I think I've worked it out.

The plane lands and I make my way to the exit. My phone lights up with messages and notifications, but one name sticks out.

Brody Waite. **My driver will pick you up.**

I follow the directions in the message. A driver is indeed waiting.

All the way to Brody's office, I make calls. My clients are confused. I don't have many answers. I should've waited, spared them any panic, until I knew how this meeting would turn out. But I can't.

The car stops. I get out and stare up at the offices while horns and sirens blare around the city. No matter what happens in the next hour, nothing but resolve fills me.

I make it to his office. I couldn't give him a definite time I'd be in, just telling him that I had to talk to him about my brother and he opened a spot for me.

His assistant, a different one than last time, ushers me into the same boardroom we were in before. Brody greets me, his expression calm but curious.

He wastes no time once we're settled at the large boardroom table. "You wanted to talk about Hayes?"

I ask the question that's risen to the top of the many I have about him. "What was he like?"

Brody's brows rise. "You're his brother."

"He might've been my brother, but he was my idol. My hero. An impossible goal to attain, according to my parents. Which I believed. I didn't really know *him*."

"I see." He settles back, his fingers lightly tapping the table. "He was driven. Wild but dependable. We went into business together and killed it. So yes, I can see why you'd want to live up to him."

I don't know what I hoped to hear, but more confirmation that I can't live up to Hayes isn't it.

Brody continues. "He also had an affair with my fiancée, married her, and then raised my daughter suspecting that she wasn't his and didn't tell me. So he was as flawed as the rest of us."

I blow out a breath. Having it laid out like that drives the point home. Yes, he was flawed. Any ideals of perfection are my own. I focused on the fact that he loved a kid he knew wasn't his like his own. But ignored that he stole his best friend's fiancée and daughter.

Just like the time he totaled the car. I kept that secret because he was Hayes. Untouchable. But he'd caused a horrible accident that he was lucky didn't hurt anyone.

Brody reclines. He's less commanding and more conversational. "I can tell you stories and stuff from college, but I don't think that's what you're here for."

I shake my head. "Remember our last conversation? You were trying to gain control of businesses I was interested in. I thought it was because you had it out for me."

"Making you pay for your brother's crimes?" His tone is wry.

"Something like that. But that's not why."

"No. Hayes talked about you. A lot. And since he's been gone, I've kept an eye on you. You've done well, married your college sweetheart, had a family, and built Underwood Equity."

"And you knew I was trying to be just like him?"

He lifts a shoulder. "He thought so. Didn't want you to

end up like him—tied to a bottom line and separated from his wife when he died too young."

That hit close to home. He couldn't help my brother, but he could help me. And when I got divorced, he rightly assumed the reason why and meddled until I came to him.

An old feeling comes roaring back to me, constricting my chest until the next breath is a struggle. After that day, Natalie came to my office and told me she wanted a divorce. She left and I was bereft. All I wanted to do was call my brother and ask him what I should do. How I could save my marriage.

But he was gone. So I did what he had done before he died. I worked harder.

Brody crosses his arms, a shrewd expression in place. "So, are you here to talk about a partnership? With my buy-in, you can hire more staff without experiencing a stall in earnings."

He's right. I'd still be the boss. And years of reaching for perfection in the work environment wouldn't be undone overnight.

I'm saying that I'm tired, and I don't know if I'm willing to do the last few years all over again.

I don't want that either.

"No. I don't want to partner with you." When Brody cocks his head, I take a seat across from him. Time to get to the other reason I'm here.

Natalie

Cans of salsa are boiling in the canner and I'm on the bathroom floor. Dad's out golfing and I couldn't hold my breakdown in any longer. A flashback to a year ago when I was in the same place and Mom flitted between me and the girls.

The day passed without hearing from Simon and now it's well into the evening. Still no word.

I wipe my eyes with the back of my wrist. My hands smell like onions and I don't dare rub my eyes. This stings enough. Mom hovers in the doorway. The girls are downstairs, coloring in the new books Mom got them for cleaning seeds out of all the bell peppers for the salsa.

"I was too hard on him," I whisper.

She steps inside and perches on the edge of the tub. The room is crowded with just us. My parents' house is a small ranch with a to-scale bathroom. I sit with my back against the sink cabinets, hugging my knees, my butt on a cushy emerald-green rug.

"I wasn't there, of course," she says just as softly. "But I doubt you said anything that hasn't been on your mind for a long while."

I stuff my hand into my hair, stopping with my fingers buried in the curls and my palm on my forehead. "That's the problem. I was arguing about what *had* happened, not what *was* happening. He asked for my help. There's literally no reason I couldn't do it."

A deep voice answered. "There's a reason."

I jerk my head up. Simon towers over us in the doorway. His eyes soften when they land on me and he shoves a hand in the pocket of his slacks. His hard chest is visible through the top two buttons of his shirt. His hair is mussed and his eyes are tired. Yet he's so devastatingly gorgeous.

And so here. At my mom's. I didn't tell him where I was. I glance at Mom. Did she call him?

She shrugs. "Last year, I helped you through this. But I think he needs to be here for you today."

Simon stands aside to let her out, then steps into the bathroom, shutting the door behind him. He takes my mom's spot on the edge of the tub.

I sniffle. "Thanks for coming."

"I'm glad I got back to town in time. I stopped at home to find you when your mom called."

I frown. "You were gone?"

"Chicago."

He was up and gone early, but he flew there and back already? "What'd you have in Chicago?"

"I sold the company to Brody Waite."

I stare at him. I can't have heard right. "You what?"

His lips quirk, but there's no teasing note to his expression. "Sold it. Done. Helena notified clients—except for Waterson, I took so much joy from that call—and I let Charlie go—with a hefty severance package and a letter of recommendation. Same with Helena. I even convinced him to contact Mr. Mellow from that startup in London that I had to withdraw from."

"Sold?" I can't make sense of it. Simon would never sell his company.

He grins, the guy I fell in love with in college making an appearance. "We're set for life, Natalie. We can have ten kids and they'd each get a trust fund, and we can still donate a lot."

I sit up straight, my hands bracing me on the floor. "You really did it?"

"I did. You can still launch Let Me Assist You. Do whatever you want for a career. I'll be a stay-at-home dad." His expression sobers. "I'm not missing out on more of my kids' lives. I'm not missing any more firsts. Every school performance, I'm there."

He's so sincere. Heartfelt. And for the first time, I see

excitement in his brown eyes instead of grim determination. "I can't believe you did it. Do you think you'll be happy?"

"I think I'll finally be fulfilled. I wanted a legacy for my kids, but all I'm doing is robbing them of memories with me. Stealing them from myself. I've missed so much and this summer only gave me a glimpse into everything we've all been missing out on. Hayes gifted me with a privileged life and to be free of his shadow and my parents' expectations—and pay it forward. I'm confident it's what he would've wanted." He digs in his pocket and produces a ring.

It's my wedding set.

He maneuvers down on one knee. "But I'll only be happy if you're by my side. Natalie Underwood, will you marry me—again?"

I laugh and hiccup and laugh some more. I don't have to think about the answer. My left hand is reaching out before I realize tears are streaming down my face. "Yes, Simon Underwood. I'd love to be your wife—again."

He slides the ring on and I sigh as the slight weight settles on my finger. It feels right.

I lunge for him as he grabs for me. We meet in a mish-mash of sitting and squatting in the middle of the bathroom floor, but we manage to lock lips. I breathe him in as I kiss him. The smell of my husband.

Running his hands up my arms, he pulls back. "Should we go tell the girls?"

"You know they'll ask about a wedding."

"What do you want? A justice of the peace? A walk down the aisle? Natalie, I'll give you anything."

He's given me everything. I smile at him and caress his cheek. "I want it as quick and as soon as possible."

Epilogue

Natalie

I sail through the finish line. My legs are tired, my body is exhausted, but my spirit is soaring. The crowd is loud, but three voices stand out above the rest. I can't see them, but I can hear them. Simon and the girls.

Aleah pulls me in for a quick hug. "Congrats, Nat. You did it. Your second half-marathon."

I grin. The first one I did was two years ago, a week after Simon and I married in our backyard, surrounded by friends and family. But I walked most of that race and thought about how different life was going to be. I wasn't wrong. It's the best kind of different. "Thank you for running with me."

She throws her arm around me and gives my shoulder a squeeze. "Us tired moms have to keep each other awake for each mile."

I sling my other arm over Rachel's shoulder. She sags

against me. None of us care how sweaty we are. We ran the whole 13.1 miles. "Thanks for talking me into this."

It wasn't hard to get her to train with me. The first year I did it, she couldn't because her spouse was gone. Last year, she did the race and trained with Aleah, but I couldn't because little Hayes was only a few months old. But this year, we all came together.

I touch my stomach. "We might not get to it next year, but maybe it'll be an every-other-year tradition."

"As long as Aleah's around to kick my butt."

"Oh, I'll be there," Aleah says. "I don't care where I am in the world. I'll be there."

Abby breaks through other runners, milling beyond the finish line with their families. "You did it, Mom!"

She throws her arms around me and I have to disengage with my friends. Abby's been running with me and Simon, and she plans to tackle a 5K next year. She inspects the medal around my neck and I spot my husband, surrounded by Rachel's husband and kids, and Aleah's husband and little boy.

While the girls and I were training, the guys formed a dad's group, which was them hanging out in someone's backyard while Abby and Kia helped watch the littler kids. Simon can form a dad crew no matter what playground he's on.

He grins as I approach, pride shining in his expression. He has our sixteen-month-old son, Hayes, in a baby sling on his back. "Way to go!"

Aleah breaks away to head toward her little boy, who's jumping up and down, clapping his little hands. "Remember to stretch." She points to Rachel, who's been swarmed by her kids. "You too."

I get encompassed in a hug with Simon, Maddy and

Abby. Hayes's ogling the bystanders, a trail of drool running down his chin into his bib and he's wearing a little white Let Me Assist You ball cap on his head. Simon had those made just for the kids.

He's my swag guy, but that's about all he does with the business beyond being my moral support. He's too busy coaching soccer and helping lead the sports sampler camps in the summer. As soon as Let Me Assist You grew until it was bigger than I could handle, he and I drew up an extensive business plan and I hired on staff. I have twenty employees all over the country and I work directly with local entrepreneurship interns—and Helena.

She's my most requested assistant and would be a partner, but she set strict hours. In her words, "Only enough work to keep me sane while staying home with the kids."

"Where do you want to eat?" Simon asks.

My first request would be to have him grill. Having Simon cook for me never gets old, but since he's been a stay-at-home dad for almost two years, going out is a treat. "Somewhere I don't have to wait on my feet for too long."

He hands me a banana and points beyond the crowd to a grassy area. "I'm under strict instructions from Aleah to keep you hydrated and make sure you stretch."

The girls take my hand and tow me to an open area. They run through the stretches with me and Simon takes Hayes out of his carrier so he can crawl by us.

The girls talk nonstop.

Abby has her legs kicked out in a *V*, but her stretch is forgotten. "I told Kia about our trip. She's so jealous."

When Simon and I were deciding on a family vacation to take before school began, we talked about going to places like Australia, London, or Paris. Then Simon talked to an old school buddy and they joked about how they should start a retired-by-thirty club. So we're going to the Caymans, and Karsten is giving us diving lessons.

Our parents are meeting us. All of them. Simon's parents tentatively reached out and after he told them we were expecting another baby, they slowly came around to the idea of me. I thought Simon selling his business would sever the ties forever, but it's like the more different Simon is from Hayes, the better they accept him as his own person and are able to accept me as well. Trent Underwood changed his tune about being retired at thirty once his son did it. Now, he boasts to all his colleagues about Simon. He even helped us set up an annual scholarship to a business school under Hayes's name.

Abby keeps talking about Kia. "She can't wait to have Dad for a coach again. Can you wait, Dad?"

Simon pretends to mull it over. "Hmmm. What am I coaching again?"

"Dad." Maddy grins. Her top front teeth are halfway down and her curls are plaited into a braid like mine—thanks to Simon. "I told her we're going to win all the games this year."

I chuckle. Simon's coached soccer, has been the dance dad in the winter and is on baby duty during swimming lessons. I thought he loved work, but I was wrong. He was driven by obsession and self-expectations. He loves being immersed in his kids' lives and nurturing other kids. And he loves spending uninterrupted weekends together as a family at our new cabin by the lake.

I run through Aleah's mandated stretches and rise. Simon hands me a water bottle. I dutifully drink. We stand back and watch Abby roll around with Hayes. Maddy's making faces to get him to laugh and it never fails.

I lean close to whisper, "Should we wait until we land before we tell them?"

Simon's grin is pure wickedness. "I say we burst eardrums on the plane when we tell them there's another sibling on the way."

My laughter rings across the lawn, but the kids are used to their dad making me laugh and ignore us. "The girls will screech and scare Hayes and he'll cry. It'll be a good time."

He entwines his hand with mine and I know we're both thinking about how life has radically changed in the last two years. We're creating a big, wild family for our kids.

Simon looks down at me. "I got a message from that reporter, the one who did the bachelor thing. He wants to do a follow-up on each state's bachelor. I set up an interview for next week."

I was so angry when I first read that article, but now I have five copies of the magazine. "What are you going to tell him?"

He leans down to press a kiss on my forehead and touches a hand to my not-quite-showing belly. "I'll have to tell him that his initial article was wrong. I wasn't North Dakota's most eligible bachelor. I was only ever eligible for you."

———

Thank you for reading! If you'd like more eligible bachelors in a North Dakota setting, you can read about Ford and Lia in Eligible Best Friend. They're coworkers who think fake dating won't lead to the real thing.

If you've read that, have you checked out my Oil Kings series? The first book King's Crown is about a widowed dad who's sworn off women to be a good role model for his four grown sons. But what happens he gets stranded with a younger woman in a snow storm and has to to share a hotel room, and a bed, with her?

Also by Marie Johnston

Standalone

Eligible Best Friend

<u>Oil Kings</u>

King's Crown

King's Ransom

King's Treasure

King's Country

King's Queen

<u>Oil Barrons</u>

Make Me Whole

Make Me Shiver

Make Me Blush

Make Me Dream

Make Me Exhale

9 781951 067663